The Magical Mermaid Portal

The Magical Mermaid Portal

Written by
Michelle Louise Gordon

Illustrations by
Lucja Fratczak-Kay

Amber Beetle Books

First published in Great Britain in 2022 by Amber Beetle Books

An Imprint of Not From This Planet

Interior Illustrations by Lucja Fratczak-Kay
Background Cover Photo by Yannis Papanastasopoulos
Cover Illustrations by Lucja Fratczak-Kay
Cover Design by The Amethyst Angel

ISBN: 978-1-912257-43-0

First Edition

Gratitude

So much love and gratitude to my incredible angel friend, Lu. You have been a dream to work with on this book, and I love the illustrations you have created. I really can't wait to work on the next book with you, thank you for being such a wonderful friend.

Niki, my faerie friend, thank you for your magic, your love and your support. You help me to create the kind of world I want to live in.

Liz, I have no idea how or why you put up with me, but I am very glad that you do, I love you, thank you for helping me to create yet another book.

Mum, I think I've run out of ways to thank you, but I will keep trying to dream up new ones! I love you so much, thank you for supporting me and loving me, no matter what. You are amazing.

Jon, my favourite merman, thank you for continuing this awesome adventure with me, I love you.

And finally, Lauren and Paige, thank you for your fan mail, I do hope that you enjoy this one as much as the first, and that you don't mind me using your names! Many thanks to Hazel, Mick and Nick for the inspiration too, I hope you all enjoy reading this one together.

This book is for all grandchildren,
and the grandparents who love them.

Chapter One

Celline smiled as she watched her cousin's eyes grow wide when she saw just how many flavours of ice cream there were. Celline had been coming to the ice cream parlour since she was four years old, when she visited her grandparents for the summer. But she still hadn't tried out all the flavours herself. Probably because once she tried the apple crumble flavour, that was the only one she wanted.

"I just don't know which one to choose!" Lily said, silently reading all the many flavours. Mint choc chip, banoffee, lemon meringue, rocky road, caramel fudge, pistachio, salted caramel brownie, cherry vanilla, peanut butter crunch, cookies and cream…

Celline smiled. "We can get two scoops each, my treat."

"Kenny will be so annoyed he stayed with Mum and missed out on this!" Lily giggled.

"We can bring him next time you come to stay," Celline promised. "A scoop of apple crumble and a scoop of caramel fudge in a tub, please," she said to the young girl poised with her ice cream scoop behind the counter. The girl nodded and reached into the freezer to scoop out Celline's order.

"I think I'll have to go for a scoop of triple chocolate and one of mango sorbet," Lily decided finally.

"Good choice," Celline said, taking her tub from the girl and licking a drip of caramel fudge ice cream running down the side.

"Tub or cone?" the girl asked Lily.

"Cone, please."

When both girls had their ice creams and Celline had counted out her coins and handed them over, they stepped out into the warm August sunshine and headed for an empty bench that overlooked the beach.

They were both quiet for a while as they enjoyed their treats, quickly consuming them before they melted all over their hands. Celline was glad she had thought to grab a couple of napkins and stuff them in her pocket before they left, just in case they needed them.

A silver ring on Lily's hand caught Celline's eye as it shone in the afternoon sun, and Celline squinted at it. "Tell me more about the faerie land?" she asked. Her cousin had begun to tell her tales of visiting the faeries inside the tree at the bottom of the garden, and how Lily had even shrunk down to faerie size to fit! It seemed very magical, and also a bit too amazing to be true, but when Kenny, Lily's younger brother, said that he had been there too, Celline wondered whether they were really telling the truth and that faeries really did exist.

"Well, in the beginning, I had to wait until the full moon, and take cakes or biscuits, in order to get in, but this ring," she held out her hand so Celline could see it more closely, "belonged to the faerie queen's father, and it lets me go to Eireaf whenever

I want. Although between school and my projects to help the environment, I don't get many chances to go. Also, my mum and dad still have no idea of any of it. I can't exactly just disappear for hours at a time. Although, my friends sometimes come with me, so we usually pretend to be at each other's houses."

Celline felt a pang of jealousy at the mention of Lily's many friends. She didn't really have any friends, having only moved to the town in the middle of primary school, two years before, when her father had passed away and she and her mother moved in with her gran. It seemed that by then, everyone already had their friendship groups, and weren't interested in including her. So she spent most of her days in school on her own, reading books, and on the weekends she went swimming and took photographs of wildlife and landscapes.

She was looking forward to going to the local secondary school in the September. She was hoping that perhaps she would finally make some friends. At least, that's what her mum kept saying would happen.

"What is the faerie queen like?"

Lily slurped some of her ice cream before answering. "She's powerful. Now that she has some hope that Eireaf can be saved, and she has her sister and her true love by her side, she seems unstoppable. Quite different to when I first met her, when she was so sad."

"It must be awful to have your home destroyed," Celline said. A thought occurred to her. "If faeries are real, do you think other magical beings are too? Unicorns? Dragons?" She looked out to the sea, the choppy waves crashing onto the sand. "Mermaids?"

Lily shrugged. "I haven't seen any dragons, other than the one at Mum and Dad's favourite pub, and that mosaic one on the theatre in town." She waved her hand towards the town centre, where the old theatre stood, bearing a huge mosaic of a green dragon. "And I've never seen a unicorn, or a mermaid, though I do wonder if they could be real too. But where would they be? I mean," she waved her hand at the sea. "Mermaids could easily be hidden in the seas, but where would unicorns be? Or dragons? You would think that more people would have seen them by now."

Celline nodded. "Perhaps their worlds are like the faerie world, only accessible through magical doors."

Lily nodded thoughtfully. "You might be right. I think it's best to keep an open mind, because, well, anything is possible, don't you think?"

Celline smiled. "I hope so." She scooped out the last little bit of her ice cream, then took her tub, little wooden spoon and dirty napkin to the bin near the bench where they sat.

Lily finished the last bit of her cone and wiped her hands on the napkin that Celline offered her. She tucked the napkin in her pocket then grinned at Celline. "So shall we go shell hunting? I promised my faerie friends I'd bring them some souvenirs."

Celline grinned back at her cousin. "Yes, let's do it." She patted her shorts' pocket. "I have a bag we can collect them in. But first," she pulled out her small compact camera from her other pocket. "Let's take a picture."

Lily grinned and struck a silly pose, while

Celline snapped a photo. Then she asked a passerby to take a photo of them both. The lady walking her dog happily snapped a couple of the cousins, as they grinned happily, their faces still bearing signs of their recent feast.

"Thanks!" Celline said to the lady as she took her camera back and tucked it safely away in her pocket. They then headed down the concrete steps from the promenade to the sandy beach to collect some shells.

"Promise me, that if you meet a mermaid, you'll write to tell me?" Lily said, as she packed her summer clothes into her rucksack.

Celline looked at her cousin from where she sat on her bed, and nodded. "I promise." It was an easy promise to make. The chances of her finding a real mermaid were so slim. She still wasn't really sure that the stories Lily had told her about the faeries were true. Although she really wanted to believe they were.

Lily finished packing and put her rucksack on

her back. "It's been such a fun holiday, I really wish we didn't have to go, but Mum has to get back to work, and I'm pretty sure Dad will have run out of frozen dinners by now."

Celline giggled. "Can't he cook? My dad was a great cook."

Lily shook her head. "He can barely cook toast. When Kenny and I decided to be vegetarians last year, he had no idea what to give us to eat. He still thinks that sausages are okay." Lily shook her head again and tutted, making Celline giggle again.

"Weird to think they were brothers," Celline said, referring to their dads.

"Yeah, I miss Uncle Brian, he was always so much fun," Lily said.

Celline's giggles subsided as she thought of her father. She still missed him every day. She wished they hadn't had to move. She loved her grandmother, but her gran's house wasn't filled with the same memories as her childhood house. But they couldn't afford to stay there after her dad died.

Shaking off the darker thoughts, she smiled

at her cousin. “I do hope you come to stay again soon, maybe one day I could come to visit you, and go see the faeries.”

Lily threw her arms around her and they hugged. “Definitely. I’m so pleased I could tell you all about it. I knew you would understand.”

Celline smiled. “I do love magic.”

“Me too,” Lily agreed, touching her silver ring bearing the seven pointed star. “Me too.”

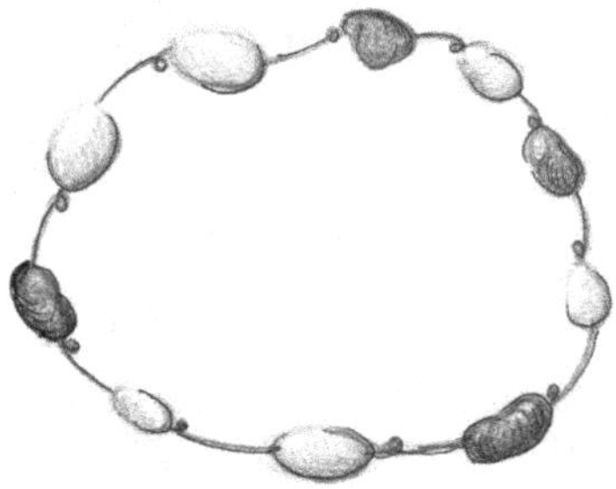

Chapter Two

"Celline! For goodness sake, stop moping around and go do something useful! You're driving me crazy."

Celline scowled at her mum and sighed loudly again. "But I'm so bored!"

Her mother sighed too. "You've had a wonderful week with Lily and Kenny, please don't spoil it by being sad now. Why don't you wash some of the shells that you found? You could make something with them? Maybe a windchime or something? It's Gran's birthday soon."

Celline sighed again, but went to the utility room where she had left the bag of shells that she'd collected with her cousin, Lily. It had been a great week, it was true. They had spent the whole time playing at the beach, swimming in the sea, going on rides at the funfair and staying up all night telling stories. And of course, there was the ice cream too.

Celline took the bag of shells to the big sink that was usually used for washing dirty boots and gardening tools, and she carefully tipped the shells out so she could rinse them. Maybe she *should* make something for her gran, seeing as she had spent most of her pocket money on ice creams.

While she washed the shells, she thought about the stories that Lily had told her. About the faerie realm, and the faerie queen. Celline wanted so badly to believe it was true, that faeries existed, that magic was real. But she still struggled to imagine it. A purple sun? A whole world inside a single tree?

It all seemed too magical and beautiful to be true in a world that had so many bad and dark things in it. It was easier to believe while her cousin was there, but now, faced with her daily chores and the loneliness that came with having no friends, it was much harder to believe.

She started to lay the clean shells out on the draining board, and tried to picture what she could make with them. She moved them about until she could see a pattern forming, and she could see that with just a few more of the right sizes and colours, she would be able to create a beautiful wind chime.

She finished washing the shells, worked out how many more she would need, then picked up the bag, folded it and tucked it in her shorts' pocket. She pulled on her beach shoes, and her light jacket, then headed for the door.

"Where are you going? Dinner will be ready soon," her mum called out from the kitchen where she was making pizza.

"I won't be long," Celline replied. "I just need a few more shells."

"You've got thirty minutes, okay?"

"Okay!"

Celline pulled the door closed behind her, and then set off down the road. It was only mid-August, but the days were already getting cooler, and shorter, and the sea air blew through Celline's thin jacket. She breathed in the salty air and smiled. Perhaps her mum had been right, she just needed to do something useful.

A few minutes later, Celline crossed the bridge over the railway line, then headed down the street to the seafront. When she reached the beach, she kicked off her shoes, and left them by the concrete steps where they wouldn't get washed away. As she made her way to the water, her feet were sinking into the soft, deep sand. The yellow grittiness went in between her toes and rubbed against the soft undersides of her feet. It always intrigued her that of all the many colours of the tiny particles of quartz and shells that made up the sand, the overall colour was yellow. Why yellow? Why not red? Or blue?

Her long brown hair whipped around her face in the sea breeze, and she knew she should have tied it up. It would be a nightmare to detangle later. She tucked it into her jacket as best she could, and kept walking up the beach towards the less populated end. Her gaze was trained on the sand beneath her. She knew exactly what shells she needed, she just hoped she would find them. Her eyes scanned the sand like a magpie searching for a shiny treasure. The waves lapped over her toes and she jumped back at the shock of the cold. The water was warmer now than it had been at the beginning of summer but it was still very chilly.

Celline paced up and down the water's edge, and every now and then, she bent down to collect a shell, putting it carefully in her bag. The waves were drawing in, and kept lapping over her toes, but she was beginning to get used to the temperature. There was something strangely comforting about the sea, she always felt at home when swimming in it, or just walking alongside it.

Celline looked at the collection of shells in her bag and she hoped that her mum would let her use her dad's hand drill to put the holes in the shells so she could string them together. Last time, her mum had insisted on doing it for her. But she was eleven now, and perfectly capable of carefully using a hand drill by herself.

The sudden, loud call of a seagull directly

overhead made her jump, and as she looked up, she thought she saw someone swimming in the sea. She squinted at the waves, wondering if it had been a trick of the light. It really wasn't a great day for swimming. The sea was rough, and she knew that the riptides were strong. She glanced up and down the beach, but didn't see anyone else there, or anyone's clothes. She looked back out to sea, but couldn't see anyone among the waves. She shrugged to herself. Maybe she had imagined it.

Celline glanced at her watch and sighed. She had to go. Otherwise her mum would get angry with her again.

She turned on her heel to head up the beach to the steps to get her shoes, when something caught her eye. Something had shone in the late evening sun amongst some seaweed.

She went over to it and crouched down. She didn't want to touch the seaweed, because it was slimy and gross looking, so she picked up a bit of driftwood and poked at it until the shining object fell free of the slimy green pods.

She picked up the object and frowned. It was a

very odd pearl bracelet. She smoothed the beads between her fingers. Some of the pearls shone beautifully, but some were black and shrivelled. Maybe they weren't pearls? Celline wasn't sure. But what she was sure of, was that it would make a great addition to her wind chimes.

She was also sure that if she didn't run, she would be very late for dinner.

"Are you excited to go to the big school, Celline?"

Celline looked up from her plate of mashed potatoes and lamb chop at her gran and tried to smile. "Yes, Gran, I'm really looking forward to it." She was lying, of course, and she knew her gran could tell. But her words were meant to appease her mother.

"See, Doris? She'll be fine," her gran said to her mum.

Celline's mother nodded, but Celline could tell that she was worried.

"You'll have a gang of friends in no time," her gran said cheerfully, eating her mash with gusto.

Celline couldn't help but smile at her gran's enthusiasm. Her mother's mash was not her best dish. It still had lumpy bits, and some weird little black bits in it. Celline pushed it around her plate, ate some of the lamb then asked to be excused.

Her mother frowned, looking at Celline's plate, then sighed and nodded. Celline pushed her chair back and went around the table to kiss her gran on the cheek before heading upstairs to her bedroom.

Instead of turning on her main light, Celline switched on a revolving light that projected underwater scenes on the walls. She flopped onto her bed and watched the fish floating past. She wondered what it would be like to live in the sea, swimming all day, floating along on currents, eating seaweed... Celline made a face at the thought. She had tried to eat seaweed once, it was quite disgusting.

She remembered her gran telling her stories and reading books to her when she was younger that all seemed to revolve around sea creatures, and mermaids, of course.

Celline sat up and switched on her bedside

light, then pulled out her favourite book from her bedside table. Its cover was worn, the pages soft and well thumbed, the spine no longer stiff and perfect.

She settled onto her bed, and opened it up, flipping the pages to her favourite part of the story, where the woman met the merman while looking for shells on the beach. She remembered the shape she had seen in the waves earlier, that had looked like the shape of a person. No human could have been out in those waves safely. Should she have alerted the coastguard? Her mum had drummed into her at an early age how to alert the authorities for help.

Celline shook her head. It must have just been a trick of the light. There had been no clothes or sign of anyone on the beach, after all.

"Lights out in thirty!"

"Okay, Mum," Celline called back. She put the book down and got ready for bed. She put on her favourite green pyjamas, that had tiny shells printed on them. Then she brushed her teeth and her long hair before getting back into bed and picking up the book again. She could at least read a few pages before bed, even though by now, she could recite the whole story by heart.

An hour later, Celline put the book down and switched off her lamp, leaving the sea light on, and she stared at the mesmerising underwater scenes that she had been watching since she was a baby, until her eyes drifted closed and she fell into a deep sleep.

Chapter Three

"Can you take this cup of tea to Gran, please?"

Celline nodded at her mother from where she sat at the breakfast bar, rubbing her eyes to try and wake up a little. She hadn't gone to bed too late, but her mum and grandmother were early risers, so sleeping in wasn't really allowed. Celline would have preferred to go to bed much later and wake up later, especially in the summer holidays. But she had a list of chores to do, and if she didn't get them done early in the day, she wouldn't have time to do anything fun later. She also only had a few photos left on the film in her camera, so she wanted to finish the film and take it to the chemist in town to be developed before they closed at four o'clock.

Yawning, she picked up the hot mug of tea, and walked slowly to her gran's bedroom, careful to avoid spilling any on the pale blue carpet. She didn't bother to knock, as she knew that her gran would be awake by now. It was almost eight o'clock.

"Good morning, my beautiful girl," her gran said as Celline walked into the room, her gaze still fixed on the mug. She set it down on the coaster on her gran's bedside table, then helped her gran to sit up, plumping her pillows behind her. She couldn't help but notice that her gran had become slower over the last few months, had needed more help, and was beginning to lose her sparkle. Celline pushed away her observations and smiled at her grandmother.

"Good morning, Gran, good night?" She settled into the armchair next to her gran's bed, ignoring her rumbling stomach and her need for breakfast.

Her grandmother sighed. "I dreamed of the sea, of looking for something I lost." She sighed again and picked up her tea, sipping it carefully.

Celline frowned. “What had you lost?”

Her grandmother gripped the mug tightly and shook her head. “I don’t remember, but I know it was important, and that I needed it to get home.”

Celline chuckled. “But you are home, Gran. *This* is your home. It always has been, remember? You and Granddad lived here for thirty years, and then Mum and I came back to live here when Dad died. You are home.”

Her gran turned to look at her, and Celline was struck by just how bright a blue her gran’s eyes were. Her own eyes were a light brown, thanks to her dad. But her mother had bright blue eyes too.

“No, my beautiful mermaid. This is not home. Not my real home. I can feel it, calling me, waiting for me. But I can’t get there.”

Celline frowned again, and wondered if her gran really was starting to lose her marbles, as her mother kept saying. Sometimes, the things Gran said didn’t quite make sense. Again, Celline noticed how much more frail she seemed, and a wave of sadness washed over her. She couldn’t imagine her gran not being there. She leaned forward, took her gran's hand and squeezed it. "I'll help you find it, Gran. We can find it together."

Her grandmother smiled at her and squeezed her hand back. "Thank you, that would be lovely."

Celline nodded and left the room, unable to ignore her rumbling stomach any longer. She knew that her gran's carer would arrive soon, and get her gran up, dressed and washed, ready to sit in her favourite spot in the sun lounge. It overlooked the beach and was the warmest part of the house in the summer.

She went to the kitchen and pulled out a bowl, a carton of milk and a box of cereal. She could hear her mother in her bedroom, getting ready for work. Doris was the manager of a hotel on the seafront, and she worked very long hours, which meant that Celline had to help out a lot at home.

Celline poured some milk onto her cereal and then sat at the breakfast bar and started eating. She saw a piece of paper with her name on it, and pulled it towards her. It was a list of chores that needed doing, including hoovering the living room and bedrooms, which was a job she hated.

The hoover was old and didn't pick up properly, so it always took ages to do a good job. She sighed and started thinking about the shells she had gathered the day before, and how she was going to turn them into a gift for her grandmother. She could see the wind chime in her head, but she wasn't sure if she would be able to create it. It all depended on if the shells she had found worked in the pattern she could imagine. She planned to wash them later, and lay them out on the table. Maybe she could even drill the holes before her mum got home from work, so that she wouldn't insist on doing it for her.

"Jackie will be here in five minutes, and she will be back again at lunchtime, so can you just keep an eye on your gran?"

Celline nodded as her mum put her suit jacket on, and slipped her black shoes on. It was a good thing the office at the hotel had air conditioning, because it looked like it was going to be another hot day, and her mum would bake in her uniform otherwise.

"See you later, be good!" Her mother kissed her on the top of the head then flew out the door, and Celline finished eating her cereal. She wondered if her mum actually enjoyed her job, or if she only did it because she was now the only one making money in the house. Gran had a small pension, and they'd had some money from selling their house, but her mum seemed to work a lot of hours, and everything they owned was old, outdated, and quite honestly, falling apart a little.

Celline took her empty bowl to the sink and washed it up, then put it on the draining board. She heard Jackie come in the front door, and go down the hall to her gran's room. She went the opposite way and up the stairs to her own bedroom, which was at the back of the house facing the garden. She wished that she could see the sea from her room, but if she left the window open at night at least she could hear the waves.

She got dressed in shorts and t-shirt, and then decided to tackle her most hated job first and hoover the house. Feeling a little like Cinderella, Celline pulled out the ancient vacuum cleaner from the cupboard and plugged it in. As it sputtered to life, she let herself daydream about swimming in the sea later.

After lunch, which was a tin of tomato soup and sardines on toast, her gran's current favourite meal, Celline finally escaped the house and went to the beach. Her gran was having her afternoon nap, so she figured she had at least an hour to roam free before she had to get back.

Celline loved her grandmother, and she didn't really mind taking care of her while her mother was at work, but sometimes she felt... heavy. She saw other kids from school on the beach sometimes, playing, swimming, and having fun, and she wished she could be as free as they seemed to be; with no responsibilities, or people relying on her. The week with her cousin had reminded her what it was like to be free, to go and swim and explore and get ice cream, without having to rush back to check on her gran. It had made her feel like she was just a kid again, and she had enjoyed it.

The moment the sea breeze hit her face, she

paused to pull off her shoes, and moments later, her bare toes pressed into the sand. Celline breathed in deeply and relaxed. She always felt a little lighter when she was near the sea, the breeze tangling her long brown hair, the sand gritty between her toes.

Despite the warm weather, there was no one in the water. She looked down the beach to the touristy end near town, and could see families on the sand, but there were red flags flying, which meant no one should get in the water. She watched the waves for a while and could see that there was a fairly strong undercurrent. Of course, she couldn't really explain how she knew this, it was more of a knowing than a logical deduction. Maybe she could tell by the way the waves moved against each other, or maybe it was a gift. Either way, swimming wasn't going to be a good idea.

Deciding that the tide wasn't dangerous enough to stop her from paddling in the shallows, Celline left her shoes by the concrete steps, then walked to the shoreline. When the first waves lapped over her feet, she gasped. Somehow the water seemed even colder in the muggy heat of the afternoon.

She went in a bit further, gradually getting used to the cold temperature. When the waves lapped just above her ankles, she changed direction and started walking parallel to the shore while debating whether or not to swim. Her gran had taught her to swim when she was younger, when she had spent the summers with her. Her mum was afraid of the water, and so she had drummed into Celline all the rules of water safety when she had realised that she couldn't keep her daughter away from the sea. If it was up to her mother, they would live far inland, in the mountains. But her gran would never leave these shores, Celline could tell. And her gran was a very strong and stubborn lady. Well, she had been, back when she still made sense.

While she searched the sand beneath the waters for any treasures, Celline mused over what her gran had said that morning about needing to find something she had lost, in order to go home. It had sounded like nonsense, but something deep inside Celline said it was the truth.

Celline pulled her camera out of her pocket,

and was photographing a seagull flying nearby when a loud shriek not far away made her look up from her search and squint at the figures just up the beach in the less populated part. She could see from their movements that they were in distress, so she looked out to the water and saw arms flailing around. She glanced down the beach, but couldn't see any lifeguards on duty.

Without another thought for her own safety or her mother's fears, Celline splashed through the shallows until she was a bit closer, threw her camera to the sand (quietly hoping it wouldn't get washed away) then she waded into the water, ignoring the cold as it soaked through her shorts, and when she was waist deep, she dove into the water. She surfaced a few feet from the boy who was struggling against the undercurrent, and called out to him.

"Hey! I'm here to help you, but you need to calm down, can you do that?" She treaded water and waited for him to focus on her. After having been dragged under by a friend who had panicked in the water once, Celline learned never to get too close to someone who was panicking in the water, without first getting them to calm down a little.

The boy looked at her wildly, his arms flailing, his feet no doubt kicking as hard as he could beneath the water. Celline waited until he nodded a fraction, then she swam closer to him.

"We have to swim along the shore, parallel to the beach, until the grip of the current lessens, then we can swim in, okay?" she said, keeping her voice and gaze calm and steady.

He nodded again and she reached out to him. She started tugging him in the right direction, a fistful of his t-shirt in her hand.

They swam together with the current for a few minutes. Celline was very grateful that she was a strong swimmer because she was beginning to tire, and was relieved when she felt the riptide ease up a little. She changed direction quickly, tugging the boy towards the shore, and towards the lady she assumed was his mother, who had been running along the shore with them. Once they could stand up, she pulled him up and his mother and someone from the nearby coastguard hut came running over to them.

"Oh my goodness, thank you!" she exclaimed as she threw her arms around her son.

Celline nodded, still breathing heavily from the exertion and the adrenalin that was pumping through her body. The breeze picked up, and despite its warmth, she shivered.

"It's too strong today," she said to the lady. "The red flags are flying and it's not safe for swimming if you don't know the waters."

She saw the man from the coastguard nodding, and the lady looked a little annoyed at being told off by a child. But Celline didn't care. Of course, she had considered swimming herself, but she knew how to read the water, and the tides, she would never have got into trouble like the boy had.

"Are you okay?" the man asked her. "You did a great job."

The lady had walked away with her boy, who hadn't uttered a word, and still looked a little in shock.

"I'm fine," Celline said. She shivered again. "Just cold. I should get home."

"You local? I can take you home if you want."

Celline shook her head. "No thank you, I can walk. It's not far. You should keep an eye out in case anyone else is foolish enough to try the water."

The man chuckled, and his eyes crinkled up. Celline noticed they were the same blue as her grandmother's. "Good point. Well, if you need a job next summer, just let me know."

Celline frowned. "I'm only eleven. I don't think my mum would let me."

The man chuckled again. "Ah, yeah, probably not. Well, you have very impressive swimming skills. Be safe, okay?"

"Sure, thanks." Celline walked back along the beach to find her camera, which luckily was still there. Then she collected her shoes from the steps and made her way over the road, over the railway tracks and back home.

It hadn't quite been the relaxing trip to the beach that she had hoped for.

Chapter Four

Celline was sitting at the dining table, carefully drilling holes in the shells she had collected for her grandmother's birthday gift, when her mum came home later that evening. It had taken a hot shower to warm her up after the sea rescue, and she was dressed snugly in her favourite jeans and knitted green jumper. She was annoyed that she hadn't finished her film and got to the chemist to get her photos developed, but she hoped to pop into town the next day to drop off the film.

"Hey, beautiful girl, how was your day?"

Celline looked up at her mum as she put away a bag of food shopping into the cupboards and fridge. "It was okay, Gran's asleep already." She decided not to tell her mum about the rescue, it would only upset and worry her that Celline had risked her life to save a stranger.

"How was our dear Cordelia today?" Her mum pulled a bottle of white wine out of the fridge, set a glass on the counter, and filled it more than halfway, which meant she'd had a stressful day.

"She was good," Celline lied, thinking of how her gran had continued to talk of finding lost things, much like the old man in her favourite movie, *Hook*, who had lost his marbles. She didn't want to add to her mum's stress level if there wasn't really anything to worry about. She threaded a piece of fishing wire through the shells, carefully tying knots around them the way her grandfather had taught her.

"That's looking good, I'm sure Cordelia will love it," her mum said, watching her while sipping her wine. "I was going to order a cake, and we'll have to blow up some balloons. It's a shame none of mum's friends are still with us, it's going to be a very small birthday party."

"As long as there is salmon to eat, Gran will

love it."

Doris chuckled. "She does love her fish. I'm sure we can afford to get a bit of salmon for her birthday."

Celline looked up at her mum, and noticed that the wrinkles around her eyes had deepened in the last few months. She had definitely lost some of her sparkle. "I have some money saved up from when I cut the grass for our neighbours this summer. You could use that for Gran's birthday meal."

Doris smiled, but Celline could see that she was trying not to cry. "Thank you, but it's okay. You need to save that money, keep it for something you really want."

Celline shrugged. "I have everything I need. You, Gran, the beach." She thought then, about how she would love a proper camera to take better photographs, but decided not to mention it. She didn't want to make her mum feel bad for them having so little money.

Her mum chuckled and drank the last of her wine. "Well keep it for a rainy day." She poured herself some more wine before putting the rest of the bottle back in the fridge. “I’m going to watch TV for a little bit. Do you need any help with that?”

Celline shook her head as she carefully drilled another hole in a pretty shell that had a beautiful mother-of-pearl shimmer to it. “No, I’m fine, thank you.”

A few minutes later, Celline heard the TV come to life in the living room, and the familiar voice of the presenter on the local news channel filtered through. She caught the words ‘rescue’ and ‘local girl’ and groaned. Seconds later, she heard her mother yelling her name.

Sighing, she abandoned her wind chime to go and explain to her mum what had happened.

“Happy birthday to you, happy birthday to you. Happy birthday dear Graaaaaan. Happy birthday to you!”

Cordelia’s face glowed in the candlelight of the birthday cake that Doris had just placed in front of her.

Celline smiled at her. "Make a wish, Gran!"

Her grandmother was thoughtful for a moment, then she nodded. She closed her eyes, and blew on the single candle in the middle. At the same moment she blew it out, a sudden gust of wind hit the side of the house, and one of the windows blew open.

"Wow, Gran!" Celline said, as she went to put the light on and close the window. "That must have been some wish! What did you wish for?"

Cordelia chuckled. "Can't tell you that! It won't come true if I tell you."

Doris rolled her eyes, as she pulled out the candle, and cut three slices from the simple vanilla sponge cake covered in seashell decorations made of icing. Celline knew her mum didn't believe in superstitions or wishes or magic. She was a very practical, logical woman, who believed that there was a scientific explanation for everything.

Celline picked up her piece of cake and bit into it. If there was one thing her mum did believe in, however, it was decent baked goods. And this cake was no exception. "Mmm," she mumbled. "Is this from Jake's?"

Her mum nodded and bit into her own piece. “Of course,” she said after savouring her mouthful.

“Best thing to happen to this town,” Cordelia declared. “No other place bakes like Jake’s!”

There was contented silence between the three of them while they ate their cake, and Celline was eyeing up the rest of the cake when Doris said it was time for presents. Her gran opened the gifts from them both: her favourite bath salts, and some new slippers. Then Celline presented her with her own gift, wrapped in recycled paper she’d salvaged from a delivery her mum had received the day before.

Cordelia slowly opened the paper, and her eyes lit up when the saw all the shells nestled inside. She picked up the loop of ribbon, and lifted it all out of the paper. The shells merrily clinked against each other, making a soothing sound.

Celline waited for her gran to say something, but she was silent. Celline frowned. She had spent a lot of time making the wind chime over the last week. Didn’t she like it?

“Gran?” She looked at her face, and realised that her grandmother was staring at the circle of pearls on top of the wind chime. Celline couldn’t bring herself to cut the bracelet up, not even to get rid of the shrivelled black beads, so she had tied it to the top of the chime, thinking it added a nice touch. But from the look of her gran’s face, she wasn’t so sure.

“Gran?” she said again.

“Where did you find that?” Cordelia whispered, touching the pearls gently.

“On the beach, a few weeks ago, it was stuck in some seaweed. I thought about taking it apart, but it looked so pretty like that. Don’t you like it?”

Cordelia nodded. “I love it,” she whispered. She smiled, but Celline could tell that something was up. She saw her gran glance at her mum, who had taken another small piece of cake and was eating it, seemingly oblivious to her own mother’s bizarre behaviour.

Celline frowned. “Okay, cool. I thought we could hang it in your bedroom, near the window.”

“Yes, I’d like that.”

Celline cut a bit more cake for herself, and for her gran, but she didn't seem interested in food anymore. In fact, when Doris suggested it was time to rest, Cordelia didn't complain as she often did, instead she got up straight away.

She gathered her gifts, and Doris helped her to her bedroom, leaving Celline sitting at the table slowly eating a sugar scallop and wondering what on earth was going on.

Chapter Five

All thoughts of her gran's odd behaviour left Celline's mind as she threw herself into preparing for the new school year. She was starting at the local secondary school, and though she hadn't admitted it to her mum or gran, and as much as she was hoping to make some friends, finally, she was also terrified.

For one thing, the school was big. It was spread out over a much bigger plot than her tiny primary school just around the corner, and all the different subjects were taught in different blocks. How the teachers expected her to be on time to each class, when some of them were on opposite sides of the school, was beyond her. Though she was not a fan of running, she had a feeling she would be doing it a lot in the coming weeks.

The idea of making friends was as scary as it was exciting. Because she hadn't really connected with anyone in primary school, when it came to choosing a group of friends to be in a tutor group with, Celline had left it up to the teacher to put her in a group because she had no preference.

She'd ended up in a group with three other girls who had been close friends for years, and had no interest in including her.

So it would be a completely new start.

"Do they feel comfortable?"

Celline snapped out of her thoughts to look up at her mum, who was looking at her expectantly. She looked down at the shiny black boots on her feet, and she wiggled her toes a little, then shrugged. "I think so."

"Walk around a bit," Doris suggested.

Celline got up and walked around the only shoe shop in town. The shoe shop was quite old fashioned, and the boots on her feet could be kindly described as 'sturdy', but Celline couldn't complain, she knew that her mum didn't have the extra money for anything cooler. As she walked in an exaggerated circle back to the stool, she shrugged again, this time to herself. At least they seemed comfortable. They needed to be, with all the running to classes.

"Yeah, they're good," she said to her mum, as she sat down and started undoing the laces.

Doris smiled. "Good. That's everything then, uniform, shoes, bag."

"And stationery?" Celline said hopefully. "I brought my own money with me, could I get some new pens and notebooks? I need stuff for maths too."

Celline's mum took the boots, put them in the box, and nodded. "Of course. I need to get to work, but here," she reached into her handbag and pulled out her purse. "Put this towards it." She handed Celline a five pound note. "Then head home, Jackie will be waiting for you to take over with Gran." She picked up the shoebox. "I'll get these and bring them home later."

Celline took the money and put it in her coin purse. "Thank you, Mum!" She put her summer shoes back on, and then hopped up, kissed her mum on the cheek and all but ran to the stationery shop.

The moon was so bright, Celline was finding it difficult to sleep. It didn't help that it was her first day at her new school in the morning too. She tossed and turned for a while longer, then finally, just before midnight, she gave up, and decided to get herself some warm milk, like her mum used to make her when she couldn't sleep when she was little.

She opened her door as quietly as possible, so that she wouldn't wake her mother, who was in the room across the hall, then went downstairs to the kitchen. She was surprised to see a light on in her gran's room as she passed, so she pushed the door open a bit further, to check she was okay.

Her eyes widened when she saw that her gran was dressed and wrapping a head scarf over her hair.

"Gran?" she whispered loudly, not wanting

the frighten her. Her gran still jumped a little, and turned to look at her. She didn't looked scared, however, she looked... guilty.

"What's wrong? Why are you dressed? It's very late."

Cordelia sighed. "I was hoping I wouldn't wake anyone." She looked down at her wrist, and Celline was surprised to see the pearl bracelet that she had put on the wind chime, was now adorning her gran's hand.

"Gran?" Celline said again. "What's going on?"

"I'll tell you, but we must hurry, I'll explain on the way."

"On the way? But it's the middle of the night!" Her gran had also not left the house in months, other than to visit the doctor. Where had she suddenly got the energy from to go on an adventure in the middle of the night? "Shall I wake Mum? Are you ill?"

"No, no, I'm not ill, there is just somewhere I must go. Your mother wouldn't understand, please don't wake her."

"Okay," Celline said, curiosity getting the

better of her. “Let me put some jeans on, and a jumper.”

Her gran nodded, and slipped her feet into her shoes.

Celline hurried quietly back upstairs to her room and slipped her clothes on over her pyjamas. Then she hurried back down, only to find her grandmother was already waiting by the door. How had she suddenly become so quick and agile? It normally took her forever to walk from room to room, and she usually needed assistance.

Celline grabbed her coat from the hook, then quietly opened the door. They slipped out into the moonlit night, and Celline locked the door behind them. With more speed than she expected, her gran set off down the road, and Celline wasn’t too surprised to note that they were heading for the beach.

Chapter Six

"Gran! Slow down! You're going to fall over," Celline was a little out of breath as she tried to keep up with her gran's brisk pace. Her gran chuckled but did not slow down.

"Keep up, sweet child, we must get there quickly."

"You said you'd explain," Celline complained. "Why are we going to the beach in the middle of the night?"

"Because the moon is full, of course."

Celline's eyes widened. It was official, her gran had completely lost her marbles.

"The moon?" Celline said, looking up at the

bright orb in the otherwise black sky. "I don't understand."

"The full moon is magic, and it helps with the transformation."

Celline was even more confused now, but when her gran mentioned transformation, it reminded her of Lily turning into a faerie. Hadn't she said that was during the full moon?

Celline's heart skipped a beat. "Gran, are you a faerie?" she asked, feeling ridiculous, but hopeful at the same time.

Cordelia's raucous laughter, deafening in the silence of the dark street as they headed towards the small bridge over the railway tracks, made her heart sink, and she lowered her head, feeling foolish.

"Of course not, child. Do I look like a faerie?" Her gran paused and Celline looked at her, her blue eyes sparkling in the moonlight.

"Sort of," Celline answered truthfully.

Cordelia laughed again, and Celline marvelled at the sound she had not heard since she was much younger, when her grandfather and her father were still alive.

In what seemed like no time at all, they reached the road and crossed it to the wide walkway along the beach. With uncharacteristic agility, Celline's gran slipped off her shoes, and then walked down the concrete steps and straight across the sand towards the waves.

Celline slipped off her own shoes, then picked up both pairs and put them on top of the concrete steps before running down the beach to her gran, who was now nearing the water's edge.

"Wait!" she called out, reaching out to stop her gran before her bare toes could touch the water. "What are you doing? The water is cold, you'll catch your death." Celline knew she sounded just like her mum in that moment, but she didn't care. She would feel awful if anything bad happened to her gran, and her mum would be devastated.

Cordelia sighed and took her granddaughter's hands in her own.

"My dear, sweet child. If it weren't for you, I would never have found my way home." She looked down at the bracelet on her wrist. "It's time for me to return to the seas. It has been so long, but hopefully they will remember me."

Celline noticed that as well as the pearl bracelet, her gran was wearing her favourite ring. It was silver, with a blue opal set in the middle, that shimmered in the light of the full moon. “I don’t understand, Gran. Go home? But you *were* home, a few minutes ago. You can’t go in the sea, it’s too cold.”

Just then, a wave lapped over their feet, taking them by surprise. But although the cold water made Celline jump and let out a shriek, her gran simply stood her ground and smiled.

“My sweet child. It has been such a very long time, but now, I must return home.”

“You said that already,” Celline said impatiently. “What do you mean?”

“I’m a mermaid, my dear. Or at least, I was once.”

Celline’s eyes widened and her mouth fell open. “What? A mermaid? How, how, how...?”

“I came to the land many moons ago, as many merfolk do, when they are young. And I lost my way to get home, here on the beach.” She touched the bracelet again. “It was while I was searching for it that I met your grandfather. He worked for the coastguard." Cordelia chuckled, clearly seeing a younger version of her grandfather in her memories. "Goodness, he was so handsome, and somehow he made me forget that I was looking for my way home. We had a whirlwind courtship, got married, and then had your mother. I told her all about my home under the water, but both she and your grandfather thought they were fanciful tales, of course."

Celline didn't know what to say, in fact, her mouth was still gaping open.

"Then just the other week, you gave me this. And now, I can finally go home."

Celline frowned and looked at the pearl bracelet. "I don't understand."

"Within each pearl, is the magic of transformation. Just as each one began as a tiny grain of sand that transformed into this beautiful, iridescent bead, each one contains the power to transform the human body into a mermaid."

"Really?" Celline whispered. A cloud covered the moon, and she shivered in the cool breeze.

"Yes, all I need to do is wade in a bit deeper, and hold one of the pearls. Then I will be a mermaid once again." Her grandmother let out a girlish giggle. "Oh to swim again! To see my home!" She gripped a pearl between her forefinger and thumb, and started to wade into the sea.

"Gran, wait! How long will you be? Will you come back?" Fear gripped Celline's heart at the thought of never seeing her grandmother again. And what would her mum say?

"I don't know, my sweet child. Once I transform, I may not be able to change back. And I may not want to."

Tears began to run down Celline's face, and she started to shiver, the cold water lapping her ankles making her feel cold inside. "I don't want you to go," she said, her voice breaking.

"I must!" Cordelia replied. "You will be fine."

Without another word, her gran waded further still, the waves now lapping at her knees. The moon emerged from the clouds and shone down on her, but when nothing happened after a few moments, Celline wiped her tears away with her sleeve, her heart lifting. Perhaps there was no magic? Perhaps her gran wasn't a mermaid? She waded in until she was just behind her gran.

"Let's go home, Gran," she said gently. She just hoped that her gran wouldn't get ill from her dip in the sea and she could sneak her back into the house without waking her mum.

After a few moments, her grandmother sighed and turned to face her. "There's not enough magic left in it," she said, twisting the pearls around her wrist. "An old lady like me must need rather a lot to transform." She sighed again. Then she looked down at Celline. "But you, you're young enough, it will work for you!"

Celline stepped back as the cold waves lapped over her knees, making her flinch. "Me? Become a mermaid? Oh, Gran, I think this has gone far enough," she said, repeating a phrase her mother often used when she pushed her too far. "Let's go home." She shivered in her thin jacket and soggy jeans, and wished she had insisted that her grandmother wrap up warmer.

"Child, this is no time to be serious and grown up and stop believing." Cordelia took the bracelet off and before Celline could protest any further, she slipped it onto her wrist, then she pulled off her ring and slid it onto Celline's finger.

Celline looked down at the bracelet, shining in the moonlight, and realised that the water was now lapping at her thighs, but it felt gloriously warm. She frowned at her grandmother. "What is happening?" she whispered.

"Hold onto a pearl," Cordelia urged.

She did just that, and suddenly, she felt short of breath. She tried to gulp in the salty air, but it wasn't reaching her lungs. "Gran?" she gasped.

Without missing a beat, her gran pulled off Celline's jacket and jumper, until she was dressed only in her pyjama top and wet jeans. Then she pulled Celline deeper into the water, and when they were waist deep, she pushed Celline face forward into the waves.

The first gulp of water felt better than the best breath of fresh air Celline had ever inhaled. She breathed in and out, and looked around under the water, amazed that she could see clearly, the salt water didn't sting her eyes at all. She tried to stand up, to see where her grandmother was, and found that not only were her jeans gone, but she no longer had legs. Instead, she had the most incredible purple and gold tail. She pulled her pyjama top off and found that her top half was covered in golden scales too. She was a mermaid! She gasped in delight and kicked hard to break the surface.

She gasped as she went above water, and saw her gran still standing in the waves, a huge smile on her face.

"Swim towards the moonlight! The bracelet should guide you and the ring will get you through the portal!" her gran called over the waves. "Tell them that Cordelia sent you!"

Celline nodded, unable to speak for the lack of oxygen, and then dove back into the water. It seemed like a crazy instruction, to follow the moonlight, but she found that it did indeed create a shimmering path before her. Despite worrying about her grandmother catching a cold, she couldn't help but swim forwards, as if a magical pull was drawing her deeper into the unknown.

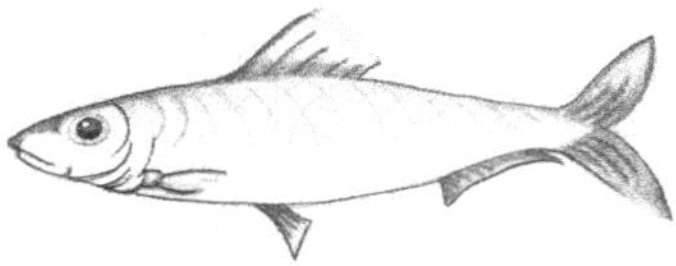

Chapter Seven

Celline's mind was racing as she swam along the moonlit path. It was a jumble of worry for her grandmother, soaked and cold, still on the beach. Worry that this was all just a very realistic dream, that she wasn't really a mermaid, but asleep in her own bed. And then there was the worry that she wouldn't be able to get up for her first day of school in the morning. But her worries soon faded into the depths as she took in the incredible sights she swam past. After a few minutes, the sandy floor dropped away, and she followed the glimmers of moonlight shining off the fish she swam past.

Through the darkness, Celline became aware

of a structure up ahead, and as it was still on the path, she swam towards it, her heart racing at what she might find.

As she got closer, Celline could see that it was a statue, a square obelisk that had a bright blue stone set in it, shaped exactly like her grandmother's ring. This had to be the portal, but how did she get through? She swam around the statue in a circle, but couldn't see a doorway, a handle or an opening.

Without thinking, Celline reached out to touch the statue, and the moment the metal of her gran's ring touched the statue, strange symbols appeared down the side of it, glowing green in the moonlight. Then there was a sudden feeling of the water swirling and whirling around her, making her hair fly into her eyes. When Celline pulled her hair out of her face and blinked, she was amazed to see a perfect circle of fish swimming in front of her, and in the centre, the water was swirling like a whirlpool. Hoping that it wasn't a trap, and that it was the right thing to do, Celline swam towards the centre of the circle, and the moment she entered, her whole world turned upside down like she was being sucked down a huge drain.

When everything became still again, Celline's eyes grew wide as she took in the incredible sight before her.

Where there was just darkness before the portal appeared, there was now an entire city built from a glimmering golden stone. She looked behind her, but the portal wasn't there, just more buildings. She gulped, and hoped she would be able to find her way back again. She wasn't even sure why she was here, it had all happened so fast.What did her gran think she could do?

Her mind whirling again, she swam forward slowly, wondering why she couldn't see anyone around. Did merpeople sleep at night too? Were they inside these buildings? Did they have beds? She had so many questions, she really hoped she could find someone who was awake that she could ask.

After a few minutes, she found herself in the middle of what looked like a meeting place, it had a clearing with what looked like a stone podium in front of it. She wondered what she should do. She had still yet to see a soul.

Her thoughts drifted back to her grandmother. What if her mother woke up and found them gone? And called the police? She would be in so much trouble.

The fearful thoughts were driven out of her mind when suddenly she heard someone make a noise behind her.

"Oh!" she said, spinning around to see who was there.

A young merman was hovering just beyond the podium, looking at her curiously. His long dark hair was drifting about him in a cloud, and his eyes were a piercing shade of blue, which matched the irridescent scales on his tail.

"Who are you?" he asked, his voice drifting towards her on the current. "Why are you out so late?"

"I'm Celline, and I just got here," she replied.

"Just got here from where?" the boy asked, still looking at her curiously.

"The beach," she said waving her hand back to where the portal had been. "My grandmother made me come because the pearls weren't strong enough to transform her."

The boy gasped. “Land? You’re a land-dweller?”

Celline nodded. “Yes, I put on this bracelet,” she held out her wrist for him to see, “and I changed into a mermaid.”

The boy’s eyes were so wide, and he was so still, Celline was afraid he had gone into shock. “Are you okay?” she asked after several moments of silence.

Without answering, the boy suddenly darted to the left, and before Celline could protest, he had grabbed a huge shell from the podium, and he blew into it.

The sound reverberated through the water, making Celline cover her ears and shriek slightly.

He blew it again, the low tone shaking through Celline’s body. Within a few moments, Celline could see lights appearing in the buildings around them, and she wondered what sort of lights would work underwater. But before she could think about it too much, dozens of merpeople began emerging from the buildings, and congregating in the clearing.

A mermaid emerged from the biggest building,

and Celline could see a scowl on her regal face. She guessed that she was the leader.

"Lir!" she said sharply to the boy. "What is the meaning of this? It is the middle of the night!"

Lir gestured towards Celline, who was now feeling completely terrified.

The mermaid glared at Celline, making her want to swim back a little. "Who are you?"

"Celline," she replied timidly. "I'm so sorry to bother you all, I don't even really know what I'm doing here, but my grandmother put this bracelet on me, and gave me her ring," she held up her hand and quick as lightning, the mermaid grabbed her hand and peered at the jewellery. A gasp emerged from her lips as she studied the ring.

"Cordelia?" she said, making a few of the merpeople gathered around them also gasp.

Celline nodded. "Yes, that's my gran! How did you know?"

The mermaid's scowl turned into a smile, and Celline felt a little more reassured that she was going to be friendly.

"She was my best friend." The mermaid shook

her head. "But that was many, many moons ago."

Celline frowned. How could this young-looking mermaid have been friends with her grandmother when she was younger? It didn't make any sense. But somehow she knew better than to ask. The more important question, was how she would get home again.

"She wanted to come," Celline said. "But there wasn't enough magic in the pearls to transform her. She said that you need more magic to transform older people."

The mermaid nodded. "She is right. There is, of course, a great deal of magic within every pearl. But the longer you have been human, the harder it is to transform, as much more magic and energy is needed."

"Is it possible for her to come?" Celline asked, remembering the excitement on her gran's face, and then the disappointment when it didn't work.

The mermaid shook her head. "There were only a few pearls, gifted to the Elders many years ago. All have now been used, or lost. We can no longer send anyone to the land, for they would have no way to come home. It has been a long time since we had a land-dweller among us. We assumed that Cordelia was lost to us forever."

Celline frowned. She had hoped there might be a way. What would she tell her gran? "Why did Gran leave? Why did she go to the land?"

The mermaid smiled, and Celline thought she looked much friendlier and nicer when she was smiling rather than scowling. "It was a rite of passage for the children of the Elders to experience life on land. And your grandmother, she wanted to understand land-dwellers. She was upset by the way they were polluting our world. We have always been protected here, in our city, but pollution had begun to penetrate our defences, and we were badly affected. Our numbers, once in the thousands, has been reduced to who you see here." She waved at the gathering of still curious merpeople, who were listening to their exchange, as their words floated around them.

Celline turned to look, and could see that there were barely a hundred souls there, let alone thousands. Her heart felt heavy. She had worried about the effect of pollution and rubbish in the seas affecting marine life, but of course before tonight, she'd had no idea it was affecting mermaids. Before tonight, she hadn't even known they existed. Her cousin, Lily, popped into her head just then, and she smiled. She couldn't wait to tell her all about this adventure.

The mermaid saw her smile and frowned. "Do you think it's funny?" she asked.

Celline shook her head quickly, her hair swirling back and forth. "No, no of course not, I was just thinking of something else. The thing is, um, er, what was your name?" she asked.

"I am Sedna, the only Elder remaining here in Sitnalta. Now, it is very late, and I don't wish to keep the whole city awake all night, shall we retire to my home?"

Celline nodded and after Sedna had dismissed the crowd, she followed her and the boy, Lir, to the largest building, that was shimmering in the moonlight.

Chapter Eight

Celline followed Sedna and Lir into the building, and into what she assumed was the living space. Of course, it was very sparsely decorated, probably due to the fact that anything too light would just float around. There were, however, some large, carved rocks, which Celline assumed were chairs. Her thoughts were confirmed when both Sedna and Lir settled upon two of them. Celline settled on one opposite them.

"I really am very sorry that I have disturbed everyone so late at night, I caught my gran sneaking out of the house, and couldn't let her go out alone, she hasn't left the house in years. But when the bracelet didn't work on her, she put it on me, and I was transforming before I really knew what was going on."

Sedna smiled. "It is just so good to hear that she is well, as so many moons have passed. I had assumed that perhaps she was no longer walking the earth, as she hadn't come home."

"Well, she's very old, and I've left her in the cold water, in the middle of the night." Guilt rippled through her. "I really should go, I don't want her to get ill. I just needed to know if there was a way she could come home."

Sedna shook her head. "I'm sorry," she said. "I wish there was a way, I would love to see her again."

Lir had been quiet during their exchange, but he spoke up now. "I can take Celline to the portal."

Sedna nodded to him. "Yes, that is a good idea. Celline should get back before she and Cordelia are missed."

"Is there anything at all I can do to help?" Celline shrugged. "I mean, I am only eleven years old, but," she thought of Lily and everything she was doing to help the faeries, "there must be something?"

Sedna looked thoughtful. "We do not wish to bring attention to our world, human interference would not benefit us. We shall live on far beyond any land-dwellers, as we have protected our city now from further pollution reaching us. But an effort to keep the rubbish out of the seas, and to reduce the waste that goes into the water, would be good, for the sake of our other sea friends."

It didn't sound like enough to Celline, but she nodded politely. "I'll do my best." She wanted to ask more about how the mermaids would outlive humans, but knew she should get back to her grandmother.

Sedna nodded, and Lir rose up in the water, which Celline took as their cue to leave. She followed the merboy from the building, and through the glimmering city, back to where she had entered. There was a statue there, identical to the one she had touched to activate the portal, that Celline hadn't noticed before. When she touched it with her grandmother's ring, a circle of fish appeared as it had before, a whirling cyclone within. The portal was open.

"Will you come back?" Lir asked her, his face hopeful. "There aren't any other young merpeople here, I am the youngest. It would be nice to be able to talk to someone who isn't so old."

Celline chuckled. "Yes, I will come back." She looked at the pearl bracelet, which now only had five pearls left. "It looks like I have a few trips left."

Lir smiled. "Good. I will see you again then."

Celline nodded and smiled shyly back. "See you soon."

She swam up and into the whirling portal, experiencing the same swirling tumbling feeling as before, then found herself back in the dark waters. She turned to look behind her, but circle of fish and the city were gone.

She remembered Lir's smile and his bright blue eyes and smiled. Then she remembered her gran, standing in the freezing water, and with more energy than she should have in the early hours of the morning, she kicked hard and began to swim away from the moon, which she hoped would take her to the shore. After a few minutes, she rose up to the surface and gasped in the cold night air. She saw some lights ahead, and knew she was heading the right way.

She dove back under and swam as fast as she could, pleased that she was such a strong swimmer, otherwise it would have taken her so much longer.

A few minutes later, she could see the sandy floor appearing beneath her, and she rose up to the surface again. This time, she could see a figure huddled on the sand, and her heart skipped a beat. “Gran!” she called out, hoping to be heard over the crashing noise of the waves. She swam closer, until she was in the shallows, then she took off the bracelet, and with each gulp of the night air, felt her body transforming back into human form.

Her grandmother had got to her feet by then, and was making her way towards her. Without the bracelet on her wrist, the water suddenly felt ice cold, and she began to shiver violently. When her legs returned, so did her jeans. They were heavy with salt water, which didn't make her feel any warmer. She hugged her bare chest, which was now devoid of scales and feeling icy cold in the breeze.

"Celline! Did you find the portal? Did you see them?"

Cordelia reached her then, but Celline was shiveringso much, her teeth were chattering too hard to answer. She took her jumper from her gran and pulled it on quickly over her head.

"Oh, child, we need to warm you up." Her gran helped her slip her jumper and jacket on. "Let's get home, you can tell me all about it once we get you dry."

Celline nodded and with legs feeling like lead weights, she stumbled up the beach, to where she had left their shoes on the steps. Shoes in hand, the two of them walked across the street barefoot, as their feet were too sandy to put the shoes on, and neither had the energy to do so anyway. They went over the railway bridge, and up the small hill to the house. Celline was alarmed to realise that the sky was getting lighter, which meant that dawn was fast approaching.

How on earth would she get through her first

day at school, having had no sleep?

When they reached the front door, hands still shaking, Celline retrieved the key from her waterlogged jeans pocket, amazed and thankful it was still there, but her hands were shaking too badly to insert it into the lock, so her gran had to do it for her. They went inside and Celline put their shoes on the shoe rack, and went straight to the kitchen to put the kettle on. There was a risk that her mum might hear them, but she really needed a hot drink to warm up.

While the kettle was boiling, she crept down the hallway to the utility room and quickly peeled off her wet clothing, putting it in a pile inside the washing machine. She would put it on in the morning so her mum wouldn't see her wet clothes.

Celline found some clean, dry clothes in the washing basket and put them on. Still feeling chilled, but a little better, she went back to the kitchen, and found her gran making them both a cup of tea. She watched her for a moment, still amazed at how nimble she had become, having not seen her gran do anything without assistance for the last year.

"Here, sit," Cordelia said, putting the mug down on the breakfast bar along with some custard creams. Celline hopped up onto a stool and held the hot ceramic mug in her hands, enjoying the heat. Her grandmother sat next to her, seemingly oblivious to the wet skirts that still stuck to her ankles. Celline pointed this out, still worried that her gran would get a chill, but her gran shushed her concerns and insisted that she tell her all about her adventure under the sea.

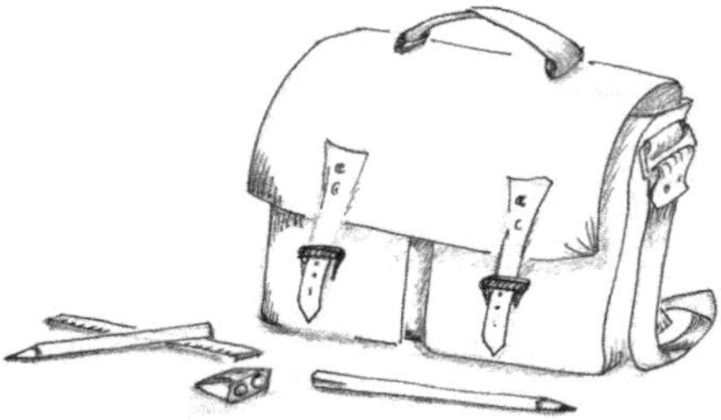

Chapter Nine

"Rise and shine! It's the first day of school!"

Celline groaned and pulled her covers over her head. Her mother's voice was way too loud. She heard the curtains being pulled back, and she squeezed her eyes tight shut against the brightness of the sunny morning.

"Aren't you excited?" her mother asked, bouncing up and down on the edge of her bed.

Celline groaned again, and her mum pulled back the covers. She squinted up at her mum who was looking puzzled.

"Did you wash your hair in the bath last night? Why didn't you dry it? You'll have to dry it before you go to school."

Celline nodded, but couldn't quite form any words. It felt like she'd barely fallen asleep an hour or two before, and was exhausted. She'd had such weird dreams...

Suddenly, the full memory of the night before flooded her mind and she sat bolt upright with a gasp.

Mermaids were real. And she'd visited their world, and met them.

Not only that, but her gran was a mermaid.

"Is Gran up yet?" she asked her mum who was fussing with her school uniform that was already laid out.

"No, she said she wanted a lie in. I've called Jackie, she's coming a bit later."

Celline felt a little jealous of her gran getting to sleep in longer. But also a twinge of guilt. She hoped her gran wasn't ill.

"Please don't go back to sleep," Doris said, heading for the door. "I'll get breakfast ready, you have ten minutes. You don't want to miss the bus on your first day!"

Celline waited until her mother left the room

then groaned again. It was days like this that she wished she was allowed to drink coffee.

Celline yawned for what felt like the hundredth time, but managed to hide it behind her hand. She noticed the girl sat at the desk next to her glancing over at her, and she shrugged slightly. The girl smiled and raised an eyebrow.

Once they had been given their new two-week schedule, they were dismissed from their tutor session early, so they had plenty of time to go and find their first class. Celline hadn't heard a word that her tutor had said, so she stared blearily down at her schedule, unsure where she was supposed to go.

"Didn't get any sleep last night?" Celline looked up and saw the girl who had been next to her smiling at her. "Me neither, was too nervous. What's your first class?"

Celline couldn't imagine the girl being nervous, she looked so confident. But she smiled back and then looked at her schedule. "I'm not actually sure. What day is it today, and what week?"

The girl chuckled, but not in a mean way. "I guess it was a good thing one of us was listening. It's week one, and it's Tuesday."

"Oh, then I have maths with Mr Jones."

"Oh good, me too. Shall we find it together?"

Celline looked around and realised that the room had already emptied out. She looked up at the girl and smiled gratefully. "Yes, thank you, I'd like that. I really am very tired, I'm not sure I will remember much from today."

"It's okay. I'm sure it will be a blur for most of us. My name is Lauren, by the way."

Celline gathered her things and stood up, then held out her hand. "Celline. Nice to meet you, Lauren."

Lauren shook her hand and smiled. "Nice to meet you too. Now let's go, or we will be late."

Celline followed Lauren out of the classroom, feeling excited despite her exhaustion, that she might have made a friend already. She couldn't wait to tell her grandmother.

"I guess your first day was really tiring, huh?"

"Whah?" Celline muttered. She opened her eyes and peered at her mum, who was stood in her doorway. It seemed she must have fallen asleep as soon as she got home from school.

"Oh, um, yeah, it was," she said, sitting up, and realising she was still in her uniform. She started taking it off, so it wasn't all crumpled up for the next day. "What time is it?"

"It's just after six, I'm going to start dinner. You can come tell me all about it."

Celline nodded, and got changed into some joggers and a t-shirt. She lay her uniform out neatly, with some clean socks and pants, ready for the next morning. Then she brushed her long hair, which was tangled from being left down all day, and deftly plaited it into one big plait. She slipped on her slippers and went downstairs to the kitchen. She peered into her gran's room along the way, and could see that she was in bed, asleep. She hoped that she hadn't caught a chill after all.

"Is Gran okay?" Celline asked, getting herself a drink of lemonade before getting up onto a stool at the breakfast bar.

"I think so," Doris replied. "Just a tired day, maybe it's the full moon, I know I always feel more tired when it's full."

"You do?" Celline asked, surprised. She didn't think her mother believed in such things.

"Yeah, I know, it's weird. Anyway, how about your favourite meal to celebrate your first day?"

Celline's face lit up. "You got fresh ravioli?"

"Yep, cheese and basil. I got it from the deli after work."

Celline's stomach growled loudly and they both laughed.

"I'll take that as a yes," Doris said, putting the kettle on to boil. "So, tell me all about your first day. I want to hear about it all."

Celline sipped her lemonade and smiled. "Well, the best thing was the girl I met in my tutor session, her name is Lauren."

"Lauren is such a lovely name, tell me all about her."

“Well we share a lot of classes, as well as tutor group. She has a little sister, called Paige, who is two years younger, and her family live on the other side of town.”

“Is she nice?” her mother asked as she added the fresh pasta to the pan of boiling water.

“She’s really nice, and she loves the beach, and swimming too. I said we should go one weekend while the weather is still good.”

“Well, it would certainly make me feel happier, you being with a friend by the water, instead of on your own. Especially after what happened the other week, something really awful could have hap-”

“Mum,” Celline interrupted. “I was fine. Please don’t lecture me again.” If only her mum knew that just a few hours before, she had been an actual mermaid, swimming deep under the sea, through a portal to another world. Maybe then she would stop worrying about a little riptide. But she daren’t say anything about her mermaid adventures. Her mum would never understand it, or even believe her.

Once they were sitting in front of the TV, their

favourite show playing, and bowls of ravioli on their lap trays, Celline relaxed a little. She was glad that her mum couldn't keep questioning her, or lecturing her on water safety. She tucked into her dinner enthusiastically, hoping that perhaps her mum had bought something nice for dessert too.

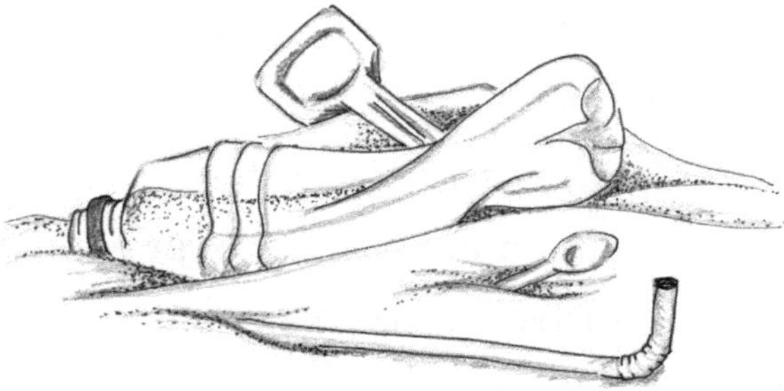

Chapter Ten

Her first week at secondary school had been a busy one, and between her homework (she couldn't quite believe how much they'd already been given), writing to Lily to tell her that mermaids *were* in fact real, and meeting up with Lauren after school, Celline had barely seen her gran. It was Saturday afternoon before she found herself home alone with her, while her mum was working the weekend shift at the hotel.

She made a cup of tea, and took it out to the sun lounge where her gran was sitting in the late afternoon sun with her eyes closed. She set it down on the small table next to her gran's chair, and the clink of the ceramic onto the glass top of the table made her open her eyes.

"Celline! Thank you, I was just dreaming about a cup of tea."

Celline smiled, she knew her gran was just teasing. She sat on the wicker sofa opposite, and blew on the surface of her own cup of tea. It was still too hot to drink yet.

"Gran, we need to talk about the other night."

Cordelia sighed, but nodded. "I know. It was all a bit much wasn't it? Certainly knocked me for six. I still feel a bit of a chill inside."

Celline frowned, that was what she had been afraid of. "What were you thinking? What was I thinking? I should never have let you go to the beach in the middle of the night, or to get in the sea. What if you'd got really ill? It would have been all my fault."

Her grandmother shook her head. "Oh no, child, of course it wouldn't have been your fault, it would have been mine. To be honest, I hadn't expected to come back, so I wasn't thinking about the possibility of getting ill. I was planning to go home, and stay there."

"Yes, about that." Celline swallowed hard. "You would have just gone? Turned back into a mermaid, swum into the sea, and never come home? Mum and I would have woken up to find you gone, no note, no idea where you were, it would have been awful." Celline's eyes filled with tears and some spilled over onto her t-shirt.

Cordelia leant forward and reached out her hand. Celline set her cup on the table and then knelt at her grandmother's feet and took her hand.

Her gran stroked her hair. "Oh my darling, I love you so much. But you know that I'm not for this world for much longer, don't you? But you're right, I should have left a note to explain, I got caught up in the excitement of seeing my home again, and I wasn't thinking. I'm sorry."

Celline wiped her tears away with the hem of her t-shirt and rested her head on her gran's lap. "I forgive you," she said. "Your home is beautiful, I would have been excited to go back there after so long, too. I'm so sorry that there's no way you can get there now."

She heard her grandmother sigh. "Yes, that is unfortunate. But I'm so glad you were able to see it. When do you plan to go back to see Sedna? I would very much like it if you relayed my regards to her, I cannot believe that she is still there."

"She would love to hear from you, but I won't take you with me to the beach again, I can't risk it. Perhaps I could ask Lauren if she would come, and then if something goes wrong, and I don't return, she can let you know."

"That sounds like a good plan. Do you think your friend will believe you?"

Celline chuckled. "Perhaps not at first, but I'm sure she will when she sees my tail!"

Cordelia chuckled too.

Celline looked at the ring that she still wore, the blue opal shining in the sunlight, and frowned. "One thing I don't understand though, is how Lily's faerie ring lets her be a faerie any time she wants, full moon or not, but we need a pearl to become a mermaid. Isn't this ring magical too?"

There was a few moments of silence, and Celline looked up at her gran, thinking that perhaps she had fallen asleep, but it seemed that she was just deep in thought.

"I think perhaps that faerie magic works

differently to mermaid magic. The faerie ring is both the key to the faerie portal, and also the transformation. Whereas your ring is just the key to the portal, and the pearls contain the magic needed to transform. It is an ancient magic, and I don't confess to remember exactly how it all works, or that I even really knew in the first place."

"Why must it be full moon?" Celline wondered out loud.

"I think the full moon amplifies the magic inside the pearls, making transformation possible. I should imagine it's even easier during a super moon."

Celline sighed. "That makes sense. It just sucks that I only have five more pearls. I'd really like it if I could visit the mermaids whenever I wanted, that's all. And I really wish that it was possible for you to return there too, even though I would miss you terribly."

Cordelia smiled down at her. "I would miss you more than I can say. But it would be so good to be home again."

Celline rested her head on her grandmother's

lap again, and allowed a few more tears to fall. She wished she could make her gran's wish come true, but had no idea how.

"Thank you for inviting me," Lauren said as she leaned down to pick up an empty plastic bottle off the sand and put it in her rubbish bag.

Celline grinned at her. "Well, when I heard that the Cambrian Water Guardians were holding a beach clean-up, I thought it sounded fun, and also, a good thing to do for the mer-um, seas."

"The mercies?" Lauren asked innocently. "What are those?"

Celline bent down to pick up some fishing net, so she could hide her blush. She had nearly blurted out 'mermaids'. She wondered if now would be a good time to bring up the subject, or whether she should wait for the next full moon. If her new friend asked her to prove it now, she wouldn't be able to, and she really didn't want to lose her friendship so soon.

"I was going to say mermaids," Celline

admitted. "But then I thought that was silly and childish, so I said seas instead." She glanced sideways at Lauren, who had paused in her litter picking to look out at the water.

"I don't think mermaids are silly, or childish. I think they're beautiful, and I certainly don't think they deserve to have all this rubbish in their home. My little sister, Paige, loves mermaids, she has a mermaid themed room."

Celline grinned at her friend. She sounded sincere, and didn't appear to think that Celline was crazy or silly.

"You're right," she said. "They deserve a clean home, along with the whales and dolphins."

"You know," Lauren said, lowering her voice as though she was afraid they would be overheard. "I think I saw a mermaid once. But it was so quick, I couldn't be sure."

Celline's heart was hammering. This was it, this was the moment. She was about to say – 'I became a mermaid, they're real' when an adult from the Water Guardians came over to them and broke their magical bubble.

"How are you girls doing over here? Need a

drink? We're all having a little break, come and join us."

Celline and Lauren nodded to Tina and followed her up the beach to where the rest of the group were drinking cups of tea provided by Dianna and Sara, who were hosting the clean-up with Tina.

As they sipped their tea, Celline wondered if she should say something about mermaids to Lauren now, but it felt like the moment had gone.

She knew she would have to soon, she just hoped that her new friend believed her.

Chapter Eleven

"What happens if your mum checks in with mine, and they realise we're not at each other's houses?" Lauren asked as she and Celline walked across the railway bridge and down the dark streets towards the beach. It was just after ten o'clock, not fully dark yet, but there was no one out, even though it was Friday night. The end of town where Celline lived was mostly just houses, all the pubs and restaurants were down the more touristy end.

"They won't. Your mum is out for the evening, and my mum is busy with stuff she brought home from work. We'll just have to stay out until morning, then head home then. They'll never know."

Lauren frowned at her friend. "Okay, but I still don't really understand what we're doing, or why we need to do it at night. What's wrong with going swimming in the day?"

They crossed the road onto the walkway and down the concrete steps to the beach. Celline slipped off her shoes, and Lauren did the same.

"Because if we did it in the day, someone might see."

Lauren was still frowning, but followed her anyway. "And that would be bad? I mean, you can't look that bad in a swimsuit," she said with a giggle.

Celline laughed too. "You'll see," she said mysteriously. She put her shoes on her usual spot on the rocks, and slipped off her jeans and jumper and t-shirt as well, revealing a very modest crop top bikini. She had come prepared this time.

"That looks lovely, I really don't know what you were worrying about," Lauren joked. She also took off her jeans and t-shirt, putting them on the rocks with Celline's clothes.

Celline slipped on the pearl bracelet, and untied her long hair from its pony tail.

"Come on," she said, holding her hand out to Lauren and pulling her towards the waterline. When they got to the water's edge, Lauren squealed when the waves hit their toes, but to Celline, the water felt like a nice warm bath. She waded in quickly, pulling Lauren with her, despite her friend's resistance. When they were in the water just above their knees, Celline stopped, faced her friend, and dropped her hand.

"Are you ready? Now, I'll be gone for a while, I'm not sure how long, but if I'm not back before dawn, I need you to go to my house and tell my gran. She will know what to do."

Lauren looked very confused. "Ready for what? Gone where? Celline! Tell me what's going on!" She wrapped her arms around her chest and shivered. The night air was quite chilly.

"How about I show you?" Celline said, a mischievous glint in her eyes. She held one of the pearls on her bracelet between her thumb and forefinger, closed her eyes, and in that moment, the full moon came out from behind a cloud, and shone onto her. She could feel the familiar sensation wash over her, and she started to gasp. She opened her eyes and saw Lauren staring at her, mouth open wide.

"What, what, what?" Lauren stuttered, as Celline transformed into a mermaid right in front of her.

Desperate for air, Celline dove into the shallows, and gulped in the salty water. When she was a bit further out, she broke through the surface and saw Lauren still standing there, in shock.

"Lauren! I'm a mermaid! And I need to go to see other mermaids. I'll explain it all later, but I thought if I tried..." out of breath, she dove under the water again before resurfacing to finish her sentence. "To explain before, you wouldn't have believed me."

Lauren seemed to come out of her shock. "You're a mermaid?! Oh my god!" she shrieked. "How?"

"I'll explain everything when I get back! Please stay here and wait for me, and if I'm not back by dawn,"

"I go to see your gran," Lauren said. "Wait. Your gran knows?"

Celline giggled. "She's a mermaid too! I'll be back as soon as I can!"

With that, she dove back under the water, and followed the silver moonlit path to the portal.

The swim to the portal felt a lot shorter this time, likely thanks to the very friendly dolphin who decided to join her. Though she had been near the sea most of her life, Celline had never seen a dolphin, even though they were often spotted locally. To swim alongside one felt like a dream come true.

When Celline reached the statue, the dolphin seemed to understand what was about to happen, because it gently touched its long nose to her cheek, made a skittering noise then turned and swam away. Celline watched it go in awe, then shook herself and turned to touch the statue. She pressed her hand to the soft, algae covered stone, the symbols lit up and out of nowhere, the shoal of fish appeared, forming a fast moving circle, and the water in the centre began to spin. She swam into the whirlpool, and moments later spun into Sitnalta.

"You came back!"

Celline shook her hair from her face, and turned to the voice. It was Lir. She smiled, "I said I would!"

"Yeah, but I didn't know if you'd come so soon, you only have a few pearls left."

Celline looked down at her bracelet, that now only had four perfect pearls, the rest were spent. She looked back at Lir. "My grandmother wanted me to tell Sedna all about her life, and to find out more about what has been going on here since she left. I was a little bit in shock last time, there is so much I forgot to ask."

Lir nodded and reached out to take her hand. They headed through the buildings, heading for Sedna's home.

Celline glanced sideways at him while they swam. She wondered if he had been waiting right next to the portal, just hoping that she would come. She blushed at the thought, and was very glad that it was too dark for Lir to notice the colour in her cheeks.

They reached Sedna's home, and entered, Lir called out for Sedna, and she met them in the living area. She smiled when she saw Celline, and this time she embraced her briefly.

They settled onto the stone chairs, and Sedna patiently answered Celline's questions, and listened with interest when Celline told her all about her grandmother's life.

Aware that it was getting late, Celline knew she would need to leave soon, so that she was back before dawn, and Lauren wouldn't panic. But she still needed to know what she could do to help.

"My friend and I helped with a beach clean-up a couple of weeks ago, and I've joined a group at school that is focussed on doing things to raise awareness of environmental issues, but it just doesn't feel like enough. What can I do to help the merpeople? To help you?"

Sedna sighed. "You are sweet, and I appreciate your concern, I do, but I feel that it is too late for us now. We have lost many of our number to the pollution, and also, a fair few became land-dwellers, when our resources became scarce." This was news to Celline. She thought her gran had been the only one, but it made sense that there were others too. "We are too few now, and the pollution has interfered with our ability to reproduce, which is why Lir is the only young one amongst us." She waved to the boy, who looked sad. "We shall continue for as long as our food supply lasts us, and then we shall pass over into spirit." She shrugged. "It is the way of many magical folk."

Celline thought of the faeries, whose homes were being destroyed by humans cutting down their trees, and destroying areas of land in order to build houses and shops. Her heart felt heavy at the thought of there being no faeries, or mermaids. She hadn't known they were real for very long, but already she couldn't imagine the world without them.

"I will see what I can do," Celline said determinedly. "There must be something."

Sedna smiled. "My thanks to you, young one.

Though remember, we shall likely long outlive the land-dwellers. So if you feel compelled to take action, do it for those above sea as much as for us below. For they need the oceans as much as we do." She glanced towards the opening in the wall that Celline assumed was a window. "We have spoken for a long time, dawn beckons, you must go, or be found missing."

Celline nodded. She really should have got a waterproof watch to wear for her underwater adventures. She rose up, and again, Sedna embraced her. There was a finality to it, as though Sedna thought it might be for the last time.

Swallowing hard, Celline tried not to cry, although she wasn't sure anyone would notice. Lir beckoned her and they left together, slowly swimming back to the portal.

They didn't speak until they reached the statue, and then they both began to speak at the same time.

Lir chuckled, "You go first."

Celline smiled. "It was wonderful to meet you, I wish we had more time, I would have liked to know your story."

Lir smiled. "I would have liked to have told it to you. But I enjoyed hearing all about your grandmother. She sounds amazing."

"She's incredible, I thought so even before I knew she was a mermaid!" Celline looked at the statue, and saw that it had the same glowing green symbols on it as the one in her world. "What do the symbols mean?" she asked, partly to delay her exit from the glimmering golden city for just a few more moments, partly out of curiousity.

Lir reached out to touch the symbols. "They spell out the name of our city, in our own ancient alphabet. If we had more time, I would teach it to you."

Celline smiled. "I would have liked that." She sighed and several bubbles escaped her mouth. "I should go now."

She reached out to touch the statue, and the shoal of fish flew into action, creating the spinning whirlpool.

"Until next time?" Celline said, still feeling unwilling to say goodbye.

Lir nodded. "Yes."

She smiled at him, then swam hard into the

centre of the portal, but she felt a weird tugging on her ankle this time, and wondered what was happening.

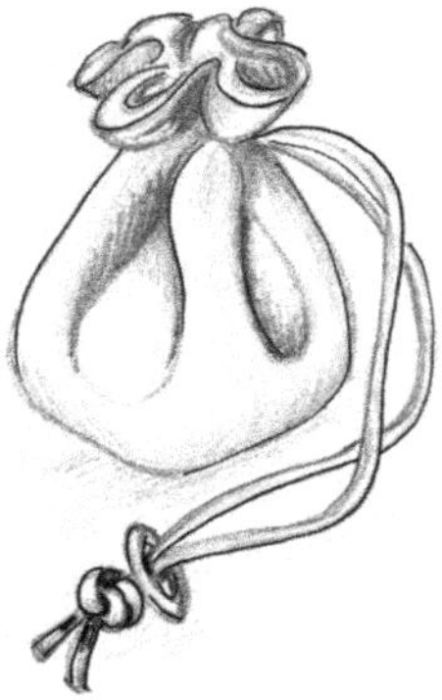

Chapter Twelve

When the world stopped spinning around, Celline found herself on the other side of the portal, with a very sheepish looking Lir in front of her.

"Lir!" she exclaimed. "You came with me?"

Lir grinned. "There is magic in place preventing me from leaving by myself, but I figured it might work if I hitched a ride. We try not to open the portal too much, so that pollution cannot get into Sitnalta."

Celline frowned. "I do hope my visits haven't let in anything bad." Her eyes widened when a thought occurred to her. "How will you get back again? Are you coming with me onto land?"

"I was hoping I might get an invite, and well, I was hoping to meet your grandmother too." His long dark hair swirled around him as he held up a small pouch that was on a cord around his neck. "Fear not, I have a key to get back through the portal, and I have a pearl to transform me back too."

Celline felt reassured, but also thrilled that he wanted to come with her, even though it was because he wanted to meet her grandmother.

"We'd better go, I don't want Lauren to raise the alarm."

Lir nodded and they swam side by side towards the shore. Celline had no idea how she would explain his presence to Lauren, or to her mum, for that matter. Where would he sleep? How long would he stay? She hoped he would stay for a while. But what if he had to stay until the next full moon? How would he live on land for a whole month?

So many questions, and yet, Celline had no answers at all.

“Oh my goodness! Celline! You’re back!”

Celline emerged from the water to Lauren’s exclamations of relief, and once she was in the shallows, she slipped off the bracelet and felt her body transform back to her human form. She shivered as the water suddenly became very chilly.

“I was about to go to your hou-”

Lauren’s sentence trailed off, and Celline looked behind herself to see Lir emerging from the water, his body also transforming into that of a human boy.

Celline looked back at Lauren, whose mouth was gaping open. “Lauren, this is Lir, he, uh, wanted to meet my gran, so he’s come back with me.”

Worried that Lir wouldn’t have any clothes on, Celline didn’t look back, but she walked over to Lauren, who was still standing on the water’s edge, speechless, and took the towel she was holding. She handed it to Lir, keeping her eyes averted, and he wrapped it around his waist.

She grabbed the other towel and wrapped it around her shoulders and quickly dried herself off.

Lauren was still staring at Lir with her mouth open, so Celline nudged her.

"Hi, um, Lir! Welcome!"

Lir smiled but didn't respond.

"Does he speak English?" Lauren muttered to Celline quietly, causing her to giggle.

"Yes, though I doubt he's accustomed to speaking above water." She turned to Lir. "Are you okay?"

Lir nodded, then cleared his throat. "Yes, I think so." His voice was different to how it sounded under water.

Celline turned to Lauren. "I have no idea where he's going to stay, how can I explain bringing a boy home to sleep over? My mum's cool, but I don't think she's that cool."

"I won't be staying long," Lir said. "I won't need to sleep anywhere. I just wanted to see your grandmother."

Celline nodded and slipped her shorts and

t-shirt on over her damp bikini before rubbing her hair dry with the towel.

"Okay, well we will still need to find you some clothes. I don't have any boy clothes in my house though."

"My Uncle Nick stays over sometimes, I think he might have left some clothes, shall we go to my house to see?" Lauren said, finally coming out of her shock.

"Good idea, can we get in tonight without anyone noticing though?"

Lauren nodded, "I left my window open, just in case we needed to sneak back in. I'm sure I can get in, find the clothes and get back out again."

"Okay, let's go, but we'll have to stick to the back roads so we're not seen. It will be getting light soon."

Celline looked at Lir who nodded and tightened his towel. They walked up the beach, crossed the road and headed along the seafront, sticking to the shadows as much as possible, heading towards Lauren's house on the other side of town. Celline only hoped they would get there before it got too light, and that they weren't caught trying to sneak into Lauren's house. Even though she had been up all night, she was wide awake, and her heart was thumping. There was so much that could go wrong, and she had no idea how she would explain where Lir had come from.

But to introduce her gran to a merboy from her home under the sea? Celline couldn't wait.

Somehow, the trio managed to get across town without raising any suspicion, and sneak into Lauren's house to retrieve some clothes for Lir. They were a bit big, but they were better than the towel that barely covered him. They didn't have any shoes to offer him, but he insisted that he was fine barefoot. He said he was enjoying the sensation of the rough ground beneath his feet, having never had feet before.

At first he sort of waddled along, almost like a penguin, but he appeared to be studying the way the girls were walking, and soon he looked almost normal. There was still something otherworldly about his long jet back hair and bright blue eyes though.

"I wish I could tell Paige about all this. She would just love to meet a real merman!" Lauren had whispered loudly as Lir got dressed behind the bushes in her back garden.

Celline sighed. "I'm just not sure how many people we should tell. If it gets out that merpeople are real, won't they try to hunt them?"

"But you said you had to have a ring to open the portal?" Lauren said, pointing to Celline's hand. "If they can't get into their world, how can they hunt them?"

Lauren had a point. The biggest threat that humans posed to merpeople was their pollution of the seas. She didn't think they'd actually be able to find their way into Sitnalta.

Once Lir was dressed, they began making their way back across town, just as streaks of pink began to appear in the sky. It would be too early to go in and see her gran, so they would have to wait on the beach for a while, until her mum had left for her early morning shift at the hotel. Then they could go into the house without causing too much suspicion. Celline hoped that perhaps Lir would tell them his story, she wanted to know more about Sitnalta's youngest resident.

Chapter Thirteen

Celline was pleased when Lauren's watch finally showed it was late enough to go to her house. She was beginning to feel quite chilly, seeing as she still wore her damp bathing suit under her clothes.

The three of them walked over the railway bridge, and up the hill to her house, after watching the sunrise on the beach. The girls had told Lir all about school and other human things he was not familiar with, and on the walk they explained about cars and trains and anything else that he pointed at in wonder or confusion.

They approached the house slowly, until

Celline could see for certain that her mother's bike wasn't in the driveway. When she was sure, she beckoned to the others and unlocked the front door with her key.

It was still very early, so Celline hoped they had enough time before her gran's carer arrived to get her gran up and out of bed. They went down the hallway, and into the kitchen, where Celline put the kettle on. She knew better than to wake her gran without a cup of tea in hand.

"I'm just going to put some dry clothes on," she said to Lauren and Lir. "Help yourself to breakfast, or a drink, then we can go in to see Gran."

Her friend nodded and got two bowls out and filled them with cereal. Lir just watched, confused.

Celline left Lauren trying to explain the function of a spoon to their new merboy friend, and quickly went up to her room where she ditched her damp clothes in favour of a pair of jeans and a soft jumper. She still needed a hot shower, but that would have to wait until later.

She returned to the kitchen, to find the pair of

them giggling and throwing corn flakes at each other.

"Hey!" she protested. "You're supposed to eat them, not throw them!"

Lauren giggled. "Sorry. Was just trying to explain what a food fight was."

Celline shook her head. She poured the hot water from the kettle onto a teabag in her gran's favourite mug, and then added some milk. She took out the teabag, gave it a stir, then picked up the cup and motioned for her friends to follow.

She carefully carried the mug down the hall to her gran's room, pausing in the doorway to listen. She could hear her gran shifting about in bed, so she pushed the door open all the way and peered around, her eyes adjusting to the gloom.

"Gran?" she said softly, hoping not to scare her.

"Celline, my love, what time is it?"

Celline walked over to the bed and set the mug down. Then she helped her gran to sit up, putting more pillows behind her. "It's still early yet, but I have someone here who would very much like to speak with you."

Her gran frowned. "A visitor? This early?"

Celline went to the window and pulled the string so the blinds opened, letting in the early morning sunshine. She looked over to the door where Lir and Lauren hovered. "Come in," she said.

They came into the room, and Celline's gran blinked at them, then her eyes settled on Lir and she gasped.

"Morgan?" she whispered.

"Morgan was my father," Lir responded, approaching her bedside and reaching out to take the hand that she held out. "Cordelia, Auntie, it has been too long."

"Auntie?" Celline asked, shocked.

"Morgan was my brother," her gran said, tears filling her eyes. "And he looked so much like you, my dear. What is your name?"

"I am Lir," the merboy responded. He sat down next to Cordelia and bowed his head. "He passed into the netherworld many moons ago. As did my mother, Ondina."

Several tears slid down Cordelia's cheeks and she clutched Lir's hands a little tighter. "My dear, I'm so very sorry. But I'm so very pleased to meet you, and to know the fate of my family. I have missed them so, all these years."

"Um, can I ask a question?" Lauren said, making everyone look towards the door, where she still stood. "How come your brother is his dad? You're so much older?" She winced a little, afraid she may have offended Celline's gran.

Cordelia chuckled. "We merfolk do not age in the same way humans do. In fact, Lir here probably couldn't even tell you how old he is, in human terms."

Lir shrugged. "I have lived the rising of five hundred and seventy six moons."

Celline frowned. "I have no idea how old that makes you."

But a moment later, Lauren gasped. """You're forty eight years old?! You look like a boy! Our age!" Celline was impressed that Lauren could do the maths in her head.

Cordelia chuckled. "As I said, merfolk do not age the same way. You met Sedna?" she said to her granddaughter. Celline nodded.

"She is the same age as myself."

This time, Celline gasped. “But she looks so young! Younger even than Mum.”

Cordelia smiled. “Merfolk can live a very, very long time. But it seems, that your parents were taken much too soon. Tell me, please what happened to them?”

Lir nodded. “This is why I came. So that you would know.”

Celline settled onto a small two seater sofa, and motioned for Lauren to join her.

“For many moons now, our seas have become cloudier. Our city is shielded quite well from the rest of the ocean, but we used to rely on a fresh inflow of water and nutrients, and when this occured, we were receiving much of the chemicals and debris that have been filling the seas. It was over two hundred moons ago when the fresh inflow contained some deadly chemicals, which poisoned my parents, and rendered those who survived, unable to bear any offspring. Most of the younger merfolk also perished, leaving only a small number left, with me as the youngest. We have no idea why we were impervious to the poison, and we have taken measures to ensure it does not happen again. But the future of the merfolk is now very limited, and I'm not sure exactly what we shall do."

Celline could see tears flowing freely down her gran's cheeks, and she reached out to Lauren, who took her hand and squeezed it.

"Some of the Elders, Sedna included, believed that we should become human, and give up on our city. But we did not have enough magic left to change everyone, and no one wished to leave a few behind. Also, many did not care to live in a world amongst the uncaring creatures who murdered their families." Lir glanced over to the girls, an apologetic look on his face.

Celline wiped her eyes with her sleeve and smiled apologetically back at Lir. Her shock at finding out that he was really an adult in a boy's body had been replaced with a feeling of shame for the human race, and deep sadness for the loss of so many beautiful beings, who were also her extended family.

"I'm so sorry I left you all," Cordelia whispered. "I only meant to come here to experience the human world briefly, as a rite of passage. But I lost my pearls, and lost my way home. Then I thought that I could maybe make a difference, educate the humans on how to care for the seas, and all who reside within her, but then I met Jim, Celline's grandfather, and I fell in love. I stopped trying to help my kin, and became human. I forgot who I really was."

"Sedna told me that you must have been kept from our city, but when we lost so many, we were glad that you were not there, that you were spared. And we hoped that you were happy, living on land."

"I was happy, so happy, until I lost Jim. Things have been a little darker since then. My body has slowed, my mind is foggy. But my memories of home are getting sharper, clearer." Cordelia sighed. "I would so very much love to go home again."

Lir nodded. "Celline explained that there was not enough magic left in the bracelet."

Cordelia shook her head. "No, the pearls are too small. I have been human for too long. A greater magic is needed."

The sound of someone clearing their throat

at the doorway made them all jump a little, and Celline looked over to see her gran's carer standing there, one hand on her hip.

"Having a party, are we? Shall I come back later?"

Cordelia chuckled. "Morning, Jackie. No you're fine, I'd like to get up now." She squeezed Lir's hand. "Wait for me in the sun lounge? Or must you go?"

"I can stay awhile longer," Lir replied. He followed Celline and Lauren out of the room, to let Jackie get Cordelia washed and dressed. The three of them went back to the kitchen and sat on the stools at the breakfast bar.

"Wow," Lauren said.

"Yeah," Celline agreed. "Wow."

Chapter Fourteen

"This doesn't taste too bad, actually."

Celline smiled at Lir who was eating the soggy corn flakes that were left in his bowl from earlier.

"Probably not what you're used to," Lauren said. She was far less giggly and shy now that she knew Lir's true age. Though it was difficult to see Lir as an adult when he looked barely older than fourteen.

"No, not what I'm used to. But I wonder if I could."

"You would become a land-dweller?" Celline asked, shocked. "I didn't think you wanted to leave the city."

Lir finished the last mouthful, put his spoon down, and sighed. "I don't. But I would also like a family." He smiled. "Seeing Cordelia, and you, and your home, it makes me realise what I may be missing out on, staying under the water. To have a partner, a child, a home... it is very tempting."

"But how would you get a wife when you look so young?" Lauren asked.

Lir chuckled. "I would have to wait a short while, allow human time to age me a little, it's true. But it would likely take me a while to get myself settled and find work, assuming that's still what land-dwellers do?"

Lauren nodded. "Yes, both my parents work. I want to go to University to study and become a marine biologist."

Celline hadn't known this about her friend, and she smiled. "I want to be a photographer."

Lauren tilted her head. "Huh, I didn't know that. Do you have a good camera?"

Celline shook her head. "No, we can't afford to get one at the moment, so I just use a cheap compact one, which doesn't quite do what I want, but I figure it's good practice." She realised then that she still hadn't finished the roll of film in her camera and got the film developed.

"I have no idea what I could do," Lir said. "But I'm sure I could work it out." He sighed. "I'm just not sure I could leave Sedna."

"We could help," Lauren said, surprising Celline. "My Uncle Nick has his own business. I'm sure he could find you some work, and maybe even some ID." She shrugged. "You would need an identity to be able to work, it's not so easy these days to just get cash in hand."

Lir looked a little overwhelmed. "Thank you, I appreciate that. Perhaps, when I have spoken to Auntie Cordelia a little more, you could show me some of the human things I would need to know? So I can decide?"

Celline grinned. "Of course. We can take you into town, that would be fun!"

"Sounds good to me too," Lauren agreed. "But I did promise my sister that I would take her for ice cream later."

"Bring her along," Lir suggested.

"Really?" Lauren asked. "Oh, she would be

thrilled! Can I tell her you're a merman?"

Lir chuckled. "Sure."

"Amazing! Well maybe I should head home to get her now, and we'll meet you at Jake's? Surely cake should be the top of the list of human experiences?"

Celline nodded. "Definitely! We'll meet you there in an hour?"

"Excellent." Lauren hopped off the stool and headed for the front door. "Tell your gran I'll see her soon," she called over her shoulder.

They heard the door open and close, then Lir turned to Celline. "Would you mind if I spoke with Auntie alone?" he asked.

Celline frowned but nodded. "Of course. I have some homework to do, I'll just be in my room."

They heard movement in the hall then, and Celline nodded for Lir to join her gran in the sun lounge. As curious as she was to know what he wanted to say in private, she respected his wishes and poured herself a glass of fresh orange juice to take back to her room, where she sat at her desk to do her maths homework. She thought of

Lauren doing that sum of the moons in her head earlier and wished she was a math genius too. But she would just have to do it the hard way.

"Hey, hey we're over here!"

Celline followed Lauren's voice, and saw her friend with her little sister, sat at the back of the crowded bakery. She was surprised to see Jake's so busy, when it was still only mid-morning, but then, his cakes were incredible. They were also expensive, and she knew that the rest of her savings, sitting in the coin purse in her shoulder bag, would likely all get spent that day. But then, it wasn't every day that she got to hang out with a cousin who was also a merman.

She and Lir joined Lauren and Paige, and a moment later, a waitress placed two large hot chocolates and two large slices of lemon meringue pie in front of the sisters.

"Sorry, we've been here a while and we had to order so we could keep the seats. You guys going to order?"

Lir looked at Celline and she nodded. "Order whatever you want," she told him. "You need to experience Jake's if you're going to decide."

"Decide what?" Paige asked curiously, as she ate a huge forkful of her pie.

"Your sister didn't tell you?" Lir said, his eyes sparkling. "I'm a merman. And I need to decide if I should stay here as a human."

Paige almost choked on her mouthful, causing Lauren to pound her on the back a few times. When she finally swallowed and recovered, Paige said to Lir. "You're a what?"

Lir smiled. "A merman. Sorry, I shouldn't have told you while you were eating."

"No way," Paige said, looking over at her sister, who nodded. "Are you serious?"

Celline smiled. "Yes, and he's my cousin. He arrived this morning from Sitnalta."

Paige's mouth dropped open and her fork hovered halfway, the meringue sliding off back onto her plate. "You're from the golden city?" she said in a hushed voice.

Lauren laughed and said to Celline. "Told you she was a mermaid nut."

"Yes, I am," Lir told Paige. "Though the gold has worn down over the ages. It is not as beautiful as it once was, I am told."

"Oh, I wish I could see it! Can I go? Can you take me? I can swim!"

"Celline's been there," Lauren said. "But you have to become a mermaid to get in."

Paige looked at Celline, her eyes wide. "You became a mermaid? How?"

The waitress arrived then, so Celline and Lir ordered drinks and another two slices of lemon meringue pie, as it was the best thing on Jake's menu.

Once the waitress had left, Celline explained to Paige how she had found her grandmother's bracelet, and how it only contained enough magic to change her, but not her gran. Then she described her two visits to the city under the water, and how Lir had come back with her, and that he was actually her cousin, and nearly fifty years old.

"Fifty!" Paige exclaimed, dropping her fork. "But you don't even look old enough to buy alcohol!"

Lauren and Celline giggled. "Merfolk don't age like we do," Lauren told her little sister. "But if Lir stayed, then he would age just like us. Just like Celline's grandmother has."

"This is amazing," Paige said. She went quiet as the waitress delivered Celline and Lir's drinks and pies, then she drank some of her hot chocolate and sighed. "I wish I had magic pearls! I would give anything to become a mermaid!"

"Most of the pearls are spent now," Lir said. "There are very few left in the city. There may be some merfolk who became land-dwellers who still possess some, but I have no idea how you would find them."

Celline thought of the four shining pearls still left on her bracelet, and wondered whether she should suggest that she, Lauren and Paige all turn into mermaids on the next full moon. But then she would only have one single pearl left. What if she wanted to visit Sedna and Lir more than once after that? She frowned.

"Will you be able to go back today? It's not full moon anymore?"

Lir shrugged. "The moon is still at its fullest

until this evening, the full moon spans a couple of nights."

"So I could become a mermaid tonight, if I wanted?" Celline asked, tucking into her lemon meringue pie. She watched Lir try the pie, and smiled when he closed his eyes and groaned.

"This is amazing," he said, eating another forkful quickly. He swallowed and nodded. "Yes, you could change tonight. You wish to come back again so soon? I thought you might want to save the pearls?"

Paige gasped. "You have magic pearls left?"

Celline nodded. "Actually, I was thinking that if you and Lauren wanted to, we could all become mermaids tonight. We probably shouldn't go to the city, because it will take too long, and you're too young to be out all night."

"So are you! But I understand why you lied to Mum and Dad," Paige said to Lauren. "So really?" she asked Celline. "You would let us use one of your pearls? To become a mermaid?"

"Shhh," Lauren hushed her. "You're talking too loud, we're getting some funny looks."

Paige looked around them and shrugged.

"Doesn't matter, they won't believe me."

Celline chuckled. "Yes, if you want to be a mermaid for a couple of hours, I think we should do it tonight, because next full moon might be too cold, and it might not be on a weekend. And besides, I'd feel better if Lir was with us too, in case anything went wrong."

Lir nodded. "I'd be happy to swim with you for a while before returning home."

"Oh my goodness!" Paige squealed. "This is amazing!" Lauren didn't bother to try hushing her sister this time, and instead joined in with her excited squeals. Celline started laughing, and Lir joined in, until tears were running down their faces.

Chapter Fifteen

The three girls spent the day showing Lir all their favourite things, and Celline wished she had thought to bring her camera with her. It wasn't a great one, but it would have been good to capture some of Lir's first human experiences. Especially when he tried ice cream for the first time. He said he had never eaten anything so cold, not even at the bottom of the sea!

By six o'clock, they had worked out a plan, so that they could meet at the beach at eight o'clock. Hopefully by then, it would be deserted, and the late summer tourists would have gone home. They didn't really want an audience.

Lauren and Paige went home to ask if they could go to the cinema with Celline and her mum. Which was a cover, of course. Celline did the same, though asking if she could go with Lauren and her family. That would give them two hours to swim, which should be long enough to really enjoy it.

Celline had given Lir some money, so he could get some food, which he planned to eat on the beach. Celline said she would have dinner and sneak out as soon as she could, so he wouldn't be sitting on his own the whole time. But he said he didn't mind.

Celline saw her mum's bike was locked up outside when she got home, and she hoped that she wouldn't ask too many questions about her sleepover, and she really hoped that Gran or her carer hadn't mentioned Lir. She had no idea how she would explain why she brought home a boy to see her gran.

She unlocked the front door and let herself in, then headed straight for her bedroom. She wasn't really hungry, having eaten so much cake and ice cream, but the smell of fresh pesto hit her nostrils and she knew she would be able to squeeze in a bit of pasta. Though she had warned her friends not to eat too much before their swim later.

Celline changed quickly, putting a clean bikini on under her clothes, ready for a quick dash out the door after dinner. Then she joined her mum in the kitchen.

"Celline! Where have you been all day?"

Celline grabbed a crisp from the bowl on the counter and crunched it before answering. "I was with Lauren and her little sister. Should I have come home earlier?"

Celline's mum sighed. "No, I'm glad you had fun, I just could have done with some help with dinner."

"Sorry, Mum, I didn't think you'd be home this early, thought we'd just eat a ready meal."

"Well it doesn't matter, it's ready now, why don't you help Cordelia into the dining room?"

Celline nodded and headed out to the sun lounge, where her gran was dozing in the last of the September sun. "Gran?" she whispered, hoping to wake her gently.

Cordelia's eyes flew open, and she smiled

as she focussed on her granddaughter's face. "Celline, my sweet. Did you have a fun day?"

Celline nodded. "Dinner's ready," she reached out to assist her gran up out of her chair, and whispered. "Thank you for not telling Mum about Lir."

Her gran chuckled softly. "Don't worry, I made sure Jackie wouldn't say anything either. I really don't think we could have explained that one to your mother."

Celline shook her head. "Definitely not. But, I told Paige and Lauren they could use a pearl each to become mermaids for the evening. Should I not have? And will it work if I take the pearls off the bracelet and make two separate bracelets for them?"

"What a wonderful thing to do. And yes, that should work. Lir will be with you?"

They kept their voices low as they slowly made their way to the dining table.

"Yes, so we'll be fine. We won't go to the city, it will take too long, we will just stay within sight of the shore."

"Good girl. I hope you all have a wonderful

time."

They stopped their conversation when Doris entered with a big bowl of pasta, and a bowl of salad. She served them and then asked how their day was. Cordelia and Celline glanced at each other and grinned.

"Oh, you know, the usual," her gran said, making Celline stifle a giggle.

"Yeah," Celline said, "really usual." She added salad to her plate, and as nonchalantly as she could, added, "Lauren's asked me to go to the cinema with her and her family tonight, is that ok?"

Doris nodded, "Oh, yes, sure, goodness, you too really are good friends, aren't you? What are you going to see?"

"I'm not sure, I think there might be mermaids in it though."

"Oh, lovely, well, have a good time. Do you need some money?"

Celline shook her head, thinking of her meagre savings left in her purse after their adventures that day. It was a good thing they weren't really going to the cinema, because she wouldn't have had enough. “No, I’m good, thanks Mum.”

“Do you need picking up later?”

Celline shook her head. “No, they’ll drop me off. I said I’d walk over to theirs straight after dinner though.”

“Okay, that’s fine.”

“How was your day, Doris?” Cordelia asked, and Celline smiled at her gran, grateful for the change in conversation while she ate her dinner as quickly as possible, eager to get back to her cousin.

The moment she finished her last forkful of dinner, Celline asked to be excused and dashed to her room, where she took out the pearl bracelet and her grandmother’s ring from her jewellery box. She slipped the ring on, then threw a towel, her camera and some spare underwear in a small shoulder bag.

She dug around under the bed until she found a jewellery kit that her mum bought her two Christmasses ago that she’d never even opened.

Using the tools from the kit, she managed

to carefully take apart the bracelet, and then threaded a single pearl onto two new strings, all the while hoping that she wasn't somehow ruining their magic by doing so. She made up the rest of the bracelets with tiny green and blue beads from the kit, before remaking the original bracelet with some larger blue beads to make up for the missing pearls. Then she put all three bracelets into a small pouch, and tucked it safely into her bag.

She glanced at her bedside clock, which was in the shape of a seashell, and saw that it was already after seven. She slipped her trainers on, put the bag over her shoulder, then went downstairs to stick her head through the lounge doorway. She saw her mum and gran sitting in front of their favourite soap opera and smiled. It seemed so boring and ordinary compared to the magical evening that awaited her.

"See you later!" she called out softly.

"Have fun!" her mum said, not looking up from the TV.

"Yes, have lots of fun!" her gran chimed in, a mischievous smile on her face when she glanced up at her granddaughter.

Celline held back a giggle. “I will!”

She almost danced down the hallway and out of the house, making sure she had her key in her pocket before pulling the door closed behind her. Then she walked quickly down the road, and when out of view of her house, she broke into a run, her bag thumping against her hip as she went.

She arrived at the seafront a few minutes later, and paused at the bottom of the concrete steps to slip off her shoes. She left them in the usual spot and then ran down the beach to where she could see a lone figure sitting, staring out to the waves.

“Hey!” she called out when she got within earshot. “Lir!”

Lir looked behind him and smiled when he saw her. “Hey, Celline! That was quick?”

Celline reached him and bent over, holding onto her knees, trying to catch her breath. “I didn’t want you sitting here on your own for hours. And besides, I was excited!” She sat down on the sand next to him, then looked up at his face.

“Thanks,” he said. “Though it’s really quite

beautiful here, I don't mind."

She looked at his face and frowned. "You look different?" It was both a question and a statement, because she couldn't quite work out why he looked different to just a few hours before.

Lir rubbed his chin, where a dark stubble had appeared. "I think maybe the ageing catches up with you when you stay on land. Perhaps if I stayed a little longer, I would look the age I really am." He shrugged. "It would make things easier, if I decided to come back to stay."

"It must be weird being an adult in a child's body," Celline mused.

"It doesn't seem weird in the city. But here, yes, I guess it would be weird."

Celline pulled her camera out from her bag. "Would it be okay to take your photo? In case you decide not to come back?"

Lir grinned. "I have no idea what that means, but sure."

Celline giggled. She held up the small black box. "This is a camera, it takes photographs. Inside it is film and when I click the shutter, a flat picture of you is captured on the film, then I get it developed, and printed."

Lir raised an eyebrow. "I understand even less now, but please, go ahead."

Celline raised the camera to her right eye and squinted through the view piece at her cousin. "Look this way," she said.

Lir looked up at her, and smiled. She clicked the shutter, and then lowered the camera and wound the film forward.

"That's it?" Lir asked curiously.

"That's it," Celline confirmed. "I would take more, but I only have a couple more shots left and I want to take some photos of Lauren and Paige when they become mermaids."

"The human world is filled with such odd magic," Lir said. "I feel sad to not know of so much of it, or understand it. All I have known of humans is their ability to destroy."

Celline was quiet for a moment, and watched the waves. "Humans are destructive," she said. "They don't consider the far-reaching consequences of their actions." She heard the words coming from her mouth and heard her mother's voice. She was sure she had said something similar when they were watching a documentary on TV. "But they also create beauty. They can be kind and loving and wonderful. And there is magic too. In their inventions." She looked down at her camera. "To be able to capture a person, or an animal or a landscape on film and then turn it into a picture is a very magical process, and I love it. Up until now, I've only used it to capture things I like, or moments, but I think I would like to use it to help people, somehow."

"You are a very wonderful, kind and loving land-dweller, Celline. And even if I decide not to return, I am very glad to have met you, to have met your gran, my auntie, and your friends. I am also very glad to have tried lemon meringue pie."

Celline giggled. "More than the ice cream?"

"Oh definitely."

Celline grinned. "I'm glad you got to try some things too. But there is so much more to experience. I do hope you consider coming back."

"I'll think about it, I promise," Lir said, patting her hand.

Just then, Celline heard voices behind her.

She looked up the beach and saw two excited figures running towards them. She got to her feet and brushed the sand off her jeans as Lauren and Paige arrived, breathless and giggling, carrying swimming bags.

"We got away earlier so that maybe we could swim longer?" Paige said, looking hopeful.

Celline checked her watch and saw it was only quarter to eight. "Sounds good." She looked along the beach and could see that it was quite empty. Then she reached into her bag and pulled out the two bracelets she'd made them. The colourful beads glinted in the setting sunlight, the pearl set in the middle. She had strung them on elastic, so that they stayed tightly on their wrists.

Lauren and Paige were already pulling off their clothes, and when ready, each girl put her hand out, and Celline slipped a bracelet on their wrist.

Lir had pulled off his clothes, and started wading into the sea.

Celline looked down at her camera, and then looked at the two remaining pearls on her bracelet.

“I’m going to stay on the beach,” she said. “In case I have to raise the alarm, and so I can take some photos. I can also look after all our stuff.”

“Are you sure?” Lauren asked.

“Yes, it makes the most sense.” Celline tucked the pouch containing her bracelet back into her bag. “Now, when you reach the waterline, grip the pearl between your thumb and forefinger, and then be prepared to find it hard to breathe. Get under water as soon as you can, and, well, you’ll see.”

Lauren looked at Paige, a huge grin on her face. “Ready?”

“Ready!” Paige shouted.

They took off running towards the water’s edge, and Celline watched them go. She lifted her camera to her eye and took a photo of the sisters running into the water. Then she walked closer to the shoreline, and she saw them splashing ahead, before pausing to hold the pearls, then they dove into the water. Moments later, Lauren surfaced.

“Oh my goodness!” she yelled at Celline. “This is amazing!”

“Look after them, Lir!” she called out to her

cousin, who surfaced at that moment.

He waved back in recognition, then went back under, along with Lauren.

Celline smiled, then sighed, wishing that she was in the water with them. But there was something at the back of her mind, telling her that she might need those final two pearls to visit Sitnalta again. To use one just to play seemed silly.

Needing to do something, she went back to where her bag was, and gathered up the clothes that Lir had discarded, and also folded and tidied Lauren and Paige's clothes. Then she sat on the sand, and when she wasn't glancing around to check that there was no one else on the beach, she was just watching the waves, hoping that Lauren and Paige were having the best time. She wondered if her dolphin friend would find them and join in with their swim. It made her feel so good to be able to give them this experience. She wasn't sure how she would have got through the first few weeks of the new school without Lauren. It was so nice to have a close friend.

A while later, the sun was close to setting,

and she glanced at her watch. It was nearly nine o'clock. She then realised that they hadn't worked out how she would let them know it was time to change back, so they could get home without getting into trouble. She also realised that they should have said they were going swimming, not to the cinema. How would Lauren and Paige explain their wet hair?

Her musings and worries were interrupted by a yell from the beach. She looked up at the waves to see Paige waving at her. She got up and moved to the water's edge.

"How much time?" Paige called out.

"Twenty minutes!" Celline called back.

Paige gave her a thumbs up and dove back under.

Celline hoped Lir would surface again before he left to go home, she hadn't properly said goodbye.

Thirty minutes later, Celline was beginning to get a little worried, and she paced up and down the sand, hoping that nothing had gone wrong. She was just considering using one of her last pearls to go looking for them when three heads popped up, a few metres away from the beach. She breathed a sigh of relief.

She had hoped to take a photo of the sisters in their mermaid forms, but it was too dark now, and the flash on her camera no longer worked. Instead, she waited impatiently on the sand for them to emerge and tell her all about their underwater adventure.

Chapter Sixteen

"Oh my goodness!"

Paige had already taken off her bracelet, and was splashing through the shallows to where Celline waited. She was so excited she threw her arms around her, soaking Celline's clothes.

"Whoa!" Celline said, laughing. "Please dry off first!"

"Oops! Sorry!" Paige let go and looked up at Celline, her eyes sparkling. "That was the most amazing thing I have ever done! We were mermaids! We had tails! And a dolphin joined us! A real dolphin!"

Celline smiled at the younger girl. She loved

that she'd had such a good time. She looked over to see Lauren in the shallows, talking to Lir, who only had his head and shoulders above water. Celline couldn't hear their conversation over the sound of the waves and the light sea breeze. A few moments later, with a small wave in her direction, Lir disappeared back into the water, and Lauren made her way over to where they stood.

"Lir's gone?" Celline said, trying not to sound disappointed and ruin the sisters' evening.

"He said to say goodbye, and that he hoped to see you again. Oh and to keep taking photos, even though he doesn't understand what that means."

Celline smiled. "I do hope I see him again too. Did you have fun?" she asked her friend.

Lauren shook her head, and Celline's heart sank.

"Fun doesn't even come close to describing it! That was the most incredible thing ever! We could talk underwater and hear each other, and we could swim so fast! And I've always wanted to swim with the dolphins. I could have stayed underwater forever."

Celline glanced at her watch. "Speaking of which, if we don't get going, we're going to be home late. How are you going to explain your wet hair?"

Lauren shrugged. "We told Mum and Dad we were going swimming, not to the cinema, so it's fine."

"Wow, good thinking," Celline said, impressed.

"It was my idea," Paige said, as she towelled her hair and started pulling on dry clothes from her bag.

"Brilliant," Celline said. "That's good." She picked up Lir's clothes. "What should we do with these?"

Lauren took the jeans and shoved them in her bag, and then put the t-shirt and overshirt into Paige's bag. "I'll sneak them back into the guest room where Uncle Nick stays. He'll never know."

Once the two girls were dressed, the three of them set off up the beach, and when they reached the main road, they set off in opposite directions to their houses. On their way up the beach, the sisters had told Celline more about their underwater experience. Celline felt a little envious, but she knew that giving them the pearls was the best thing she could have ever done.

They tried to give her the bracelets back, but she told them to keep them as a souvenir of their adventure. The magic pearls were now blackened and smaller, the magic within them spent. So they were now simply a reminder of their night as mermaids.

Going back to school on Monday felt like a shock to Celline. Going to lessons, doing maths, English and science, it all felt so ordinary and pointless. She wished that she could just be a mermaid, and live in the golden city. Throughout the day, her thoughts returned to the last two pearls. Maybe she would actually do just that. When she was old enough, she could go and live in the golden city under the water.

She felt a longing to swim and be free. After experiencing being a mermaid twice, she now felt trapped when on land.

Lauren couldn't stop talking about their swim. And apparently, neither could Paige. Though Paige would very much liked to have visited the golden city, she understood that it would have taken too long.

Finally, after what felt like a week, Monday came to an end and Lauren and Celline left their final class of the day, Geography. It was a subject that Celline usually enjoyed, but she found that she hadn't paid any attention to what her teacher had said for the previous hour.

"Hey, can you come over?" Lauren asked her as they reached the front of the school, where Lauren normally waited for Paige to come out of the adjoining primary school before getting the bus home together.

"I think so, I'll go home first and check, in case Mum is cooking or Gran needs something. I can call you?"

"Great, and don't worry about dinner, you can eat with us."

Celline nodded. "Okay, I'll let you know."

Paige arrived then, and the three of them were

only waiting at the bus stop for a few minutes before it ambled along, and they all hopped on. Paige chattered excitedly about their experience the night before for the whole forty-five minute ride.

When they reached their stop, Paige and Lauren got off, and then Celline alighted two stops later. Celline headed up the hill towards her house, walking quickly so she could get to Lauren's sooner. She knew that her mum had been missing her company in the evenings, but it felt so good to spend more time with friends, instead of just sitting in front of the TV every night, watching soaps and documentaries, or worse, the news.

Celline reached her front door a little out of breath, and saw that her mum's bike wasn't in the driveway. She opened the door with her key and went inside. She could hear noises from her gran's room, so she pushed the door open a little and stuck her head round. Her gran was in bed. Sitting up and drinking a cup of tea.

"Celline! Goodness, is it after four already?"

"Yes, Gran, school's finished. Is Mum home

soon? I wanted to ask if I could go over Lauren's."

"Yes, she rang a while ago, she'll be home by five, so you go and enjoy yourself. I was feeling a bit tired, so I asked Jackie to help me to bed. I'll get up in a bit for some food with your mum."

Celline felt a twinge of guilt. Perhaps she should stay home instead. She hadn't spent nearly as much time with her gran recently as she had before school had started.

"Go," Cordelia said gently, as if sensing her hesitation. "We can watch a movie together tomorrow?"

Celline nodded. "Yes, I'd like that." She went over to her gran and kissed her on the cheek.

"See you tomorrow, my sweet child."

"Love you," Celline responded as she left. She went upstairs to her room and got changed out of her uniform, then put her camera in her bag. There was only a couple of shots left on the film, maybe she could finish it that night, so she could finally take it to the chemists to get it developed. She wanted to give her gran the photo of Lir, so that she had something to remember him by.

She also wanted to give Lauren and Paige the

photo of them running into the sea. She hoped the photos came out okay, her camera really was quite old and cheap. Her father had given it to her for her seventh birthday.

She put her maths homework into her bag too, perhaps she and Lauren could do it together, seeing as Lauren was so good with numbers. She called Lauren quickly on the house phone to let her know she was on her way.

Without waiting for her mum to return, ten minutes later, Celline called out goodbye to her gran then headed out into the late afternoon sunshine. She was pleased that, so far, the autumn had been so dry. She hated having to walk a lot when it rained.

It took her twenty minutes to reach Lauren's house, and by the time she got there, she was very hungry. She hoped maybe they had some snacks she could have before dinner.

She knocked on the front door and it was opened only a couple of minutes later by Lauren, who grabbed her and pulled her into the house.

"Hi!" Celline responded with a giggle. "Anybody would think you hadn't seen me in years."

Lauren chuckled, "Sorry, I'm just excited. I have a surprise for you!"

"Oh?" Celline said, curious. "What kind of surprise?"

"Come out to the garage and you'll see!"

Celline frowned, wondering what kind of surprise could be kept in the garage, but followed her friend anyway.

A few moments later, they stepped into the cool dark garage, and a weird chemical smell hit her nostrils. Celline wrinkled her nose. "Eww, what is that?"

Lauren giggled. "Come and see!" She stepped through another door, and disappeared. Really curious now, and mildly alarmed, Celline followed and the smell of chemicals got stronger. When she stepped through a heavy curtain, she blinked as her eyes slowly adjusted to the muted red light in the room. She looked around and saw trays of liquid, and a string of photographs hanging up.

"Oh! Is this a darkroom?" she asked.

"Yes, it's my dad's," Lauren replied.

"Yes it is," a voice said from a corner of the room.

Celline jumped a little. "Oh! I didn't see you there. I'm sorry, we shouldn't be in here."

"Nonsense," Lauren's dad replied. "Lauren tells me that you are a keen photographer."

Celline thought of her camera in her bag, and shrugged. "I like taking photos, but I don't have a very good camera."

"What camera do you have?"

Celline pulled her camera out from her bag and handed it to Lauren's dad. He took it from her and nodded. "This isn't a bad one to start with, but to really capture your subjects with more detail you will need a better one."

He handed it back to her and she put it back in her bag. She looked around the darkroom, wishing that she could be a photographer too.

"I have an old SLR, if you'd like to use it?" he continued.

Celline looked at Lauren's dad, and her eye widened. "Really? Aren't they really expensive?"

He smiled. "It's the one I started with, I've upgraded since, and it's a shame to see it just sitting there." He waved at Lauren. "I have offered it to the girls, but it's not their thing. So, if you'd like it? I can show you the basics, and if you'd like to shoot in black and white, I'd be happy to show you how to develop film and then enlarge the prints. Once you know what you're doing, you could always use this space when I'm not working in here."

Celline's eyes filled with tears and she wiped them away quickly, feeling embarrassed. "Yes please," she said, "I'd really love that."

"See? I told you I had a surprise!" Lauren said, putting her arm around Celline.

Celline giggled. "Yes, thank you, this is amazing."

"Okay, well, let's go get the camera, and we can have our first lesson tonight, if you have time?"

Celline nodded quickly. "Yes, I don't have to be home for a while yet."

"Perfect."

Celline followed Lauren and her father from the darkroom, excitement bubbling up inside her. She had a feeling that the next few hours would be the beginning of a whole new chapter of her life.

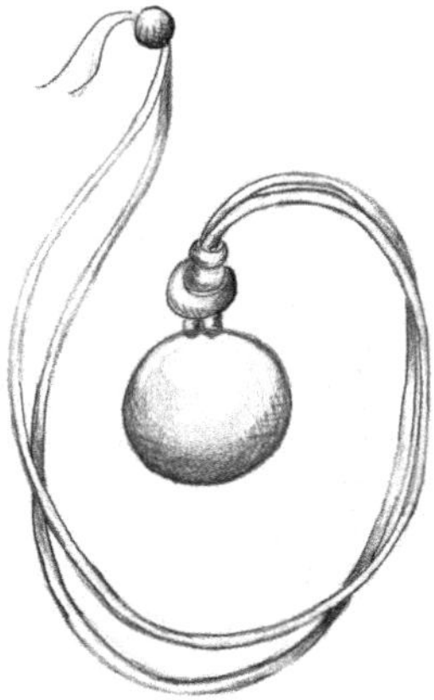

Chapter Seventeen

"So this is the shutter speed, which means how long the shutter opens up to let in the light, which hits the mirror and reflects onto the film. And this is the aperture, which is how wide the lens is open, so it's another way to control how much light goes in."

Cordelia smiled at her granddaughter's enthusiasm. "I have absolutely no idea what any of that means, but it sounds wonderful. So very generous of Lauren's dad to gift it to you."

Celline smiled at her gran, and then she lifted the camera to her eye and focused the lens on her gran's face, before clicking the shutter. "It really was."

It was all thanks to Lauren that she would finally be able to realise her dream of becoming a photographer. After receiving the camera and a short lesson from Lauren's dad the evening before, they had gone to Lauren's room to do their homework, but Celline was too excited to concentrate.

"Why did your dad give me his camera?" she had asked her friend. "It's such a huge thing to give away."

Lauren grinned. "I told him that you had helped me to see how much I want to be a marine biologist, and that I wanted to thank you, and I knew that he didn't use that camera anymore." She giggled. "I think he was just excited that someone might want to learn photography from him. I know Paige and I disappointed him when we didn't want to get covered in stinky chemicals and spend hours in a dark red room."

Celline had stroked her new camera lovingly. "I can't wait!"

"Weirdo," Lauren had teased.

"Surely there must be better subjects to

photograph than me?" her gran asked, bringing Celline back to the present. Celline grinned and clicked the shutter again.

"No one else stays as still as you, Gran," Celline teased back.

Cordelia chuckled and picked up her tea. "That's true," she said, taking a sip. "But really, why don't you go to the beach, or to town? It's Saturday, aren't you seeing Lauren today?"

Celline lowered the camera and shook her head. "Lauren and her family have gone away to see her grandparents for the weekend. And besides, it's raining. I'd rather stay here, and take photos of my favourite person."

Cordelia smiled broadly, her bright blue eyes sparkling, her face wrinkling up beautifully. Celline lifted her camera quickly and captured it. She couldn't wait to develop her first roll of black and white film. Lauren's dad had promised he would show her how.

"When is the moon next full, my dear?"

Celline frowned. "Um, I'm not sure. Hang on."

She got up, and set the camera down on the

coffee table. She went into the kitchen and looked on the calendar there for the small circles that signified the moon cycles. She found the next empty circle, which was in seven days' time.

"Next Saturday, Gran," she said, walking back into the sun lounge.

But her gran had already fallen asleep, and was snoring gently. Celline smiled and pulled the blanket higher up on her lap.

She picked up her camera and decided to go and read the photography book that Lauren's dad had lent her. She wanted to learn more about the settings she would need to use to be able to photograph the stars.

Celline smiled as she tacked her very first black and white prints to her corkboard on the wall of her bedroom a week later. The ones of her gran had come out particularly well. She tacked them next to the photo of Lir, and her two friends running into the sea. The difference in quality was vast, but she still loved the slightly blurry ones she took on her old camera. They were moments she would never again be able to capture on film.

Celline wondered if she would ever see her cousin again. There was a full moon again that night, and she was half-considering going to the beach after dark to see if Lir appeared.

"Celline!"

Her mum's voice pulled Celline out of her thoughts and back to the present moment. She'd forgotten that she had promised to help with dinner. "Coming!" she called back, tacking up the final photo she had developed in Lauren's dad's darkroom the evening before.

"Sorry, Mum," she said, entering the kitchen and washing her hands before picking up the peeler and attacking the pile of carrots.

"It's okay, I know you've been busy with your photography. Those pictures of your gran really are wonderful."

Celline smiled. "She makes a great subject. I'm lucky to have so much time with her, though I do wish I'd taken more photos before."

"Well you still have plenty of time," Doris said. "Your gran's not going anywhere."

Celline frowned. Perhaps. But her gran *had* tried to go back to her home city under the water. She remembered her gran's question a few days before about the moon. She wasn't thinking of trying again?

"Where's Gran?" Celline asked her mum.

"In her room, resting I think," her mum replied, as she checked on the chicken in the oven.

"Um, I just need to ask her something," Celline said, drying her hands on the tea towel. "Won't be a minute."

Celline dashed out of the kitchen and down the hall to her gran's room before her mum could protest. Without knocking, she slowly nudged the door open, and peered around into the room.

Half expecting to find her gran gone, she was surprised to see her sitting at a small writing desk in the corner of the room. Celline had never seen her use it before.

"Gran?" she called softly.

Cordelia quickly shuffled some papers together, then closed the writing desk before turning around.

"Yes, my sweet child?"

"Just came to see if you wanted a cup of tea," Celline lied. She went into the room and a small pouch on her gran's bed caught her eye. She frowned and reached out to pick it up.

"This is Lir's," she said.

Cordelia stood up and with a speed Celline had never seen in the old woman before, she crossed the room to grab the pouch from Celline's hands. Shocked, Celline didn't try to stop her.

"He gave it to me," Cordelia said. "A gift."

"What's inside?" Celline asked. It had felt like a pebble.

"Never you mind," her gran replied, tucking the pouch into her cardigan pocket.

Celline raised her eyebrows. "Gran, what's going on? Be honest with me, please."

Cordelia sighed and sat on the edge of the bed. Celline sat next to her and waited.

"It's a pearl necklace. It belonged to Lir's mother. She had hoped to experience land-dwelling one day, but never had the chance."

"Wait, a pearl necklace? With magic pearls?"

Cordelia sighed and pulled the pouch out and

tipped the contents into Celline's hand. It was no ordinary pearl necklace, it was a simple cord with one very large pearl tied in the centre. It was beautiful. But Celline began to cry.

"You're going to try again?" she whispered. "Tonight?"

Cordelia nodded. "I was just writing letters to you and your mother, to explain. And to try and avoid her calling the police. Don't want to waste everyone's time with search parties."

The tears rolled freely down Celline's face as she rolled the large pearl around in her hand. "You can't leave us, Gran. Please, don't go."

Cordelia sighed again and wrapped her arm around her granddaughter. "My sweet child, either way, I will be going soon. And I would much rather go home, then go to some unknown netherworld. At least if I go home, you will know where I am, and just as I was writing in my letter to you, I would very much like you to keep those two final pearls of yours, and visit me again when you're a bit older. Because I would love to see you all grown up."

Celline started to sob, and her gran hushed

her. "Mum won't understand," she choked out. "How have you explained it to her? What will I say? She'll be so angry if she finds out I knew."

"Then pretend you didn't know. I will slip out later, and you will be tucked up in bed-"

"No, absolutely not. I'm coming with you." Celline sat up straight and wiped her face with her sleeve. "I can't let you go alone."

Cordelia smiled. "I won't be alone, Lir is coming for me."

"Lir is coming? How do you know?"

"He said that if I wanted to go home, then I should meet him on the beach tonight."

"What time are we going?"

Cordelia shook her head. "You should stay here."

"What time, Gran?"

"Ten o'clock. The moon should have risen by then."

"Okay, Mum should be in bed by then, she has an early shift tomorrow. Do not leave without me, okay?" Celline waited for her gran to nod, then she stood up. "I better go finish helping with dinner."

“I’ll be through soon.”

Celline walked back to the kitchen, and found that in her absence, her mother had finished peeling the carrots and had put them onto boil. She poured herself some water and drank half the glass in one gulp. The idea of her gran going home was just too awful to contemplate, even though she knew that it was what her gran really wanted. But how would she be able to say goodbye?

Chapter Eighteen

Celline could barely choke down a few mouthfuls of her dinner, but luckily her mum seemed too distracted to notice. She asked to be excused from the dinner table, needing to be alone while she prepared herself to take her gran to the beach.

Safely upstairs in her room, Celline let her tears fall as she looked at her board of photos. She was so glad that she had taken so many of her gran in the last week or so. She decided to ask her mum one day if they could look for older photos of her gran, in the boxes that were still packed up in the loft.

She sniffled, thinking of how much she would miss her gran. Only a few weeks ago, she had felt slightly annoyed at having to be at home so much, tending to her gran. Now, she was so glad that she had seen her so much.

It still didn't take away the pain of the idea of not seeing her gran again. Though, with the pearls, she *could* see her again. But when? Her gran said she wanted her to wait a few years.

Celline took in a deep shuddering breath and pulled a tissue out of her jeans pocket to blow her nose. She needed to find a way to be strong for her gran. And for her mum. She really didn't think that anything her gran had written in her letter would make her understand. The next few days were bound to be hard.

She pulled out her favourite green jumper from her wardrobe, and put it ready on her chair. Then she got into bed, fully clothed, and pulled the covers up so her mum wouldn't notice she wasn't wearing pyjamas when she came to say good night.

Celline picked up a book they were supposed to be reading for English class at school, and attempted to read it, but her eyes were just skimming the words with no idea of what they said or meant.

An hour later, her mum poked her head round the door.

"Good night, Celline. You okay?"

Celline nodded and managed to smile at her mother. "Yeah, just tired. See you in the morning,"

Doris smiled back and blew her a kiss. "Love you."

Tears filled Celline's eyes, and she echoed. "Love you."

Luckily, Doris left the room before she noticed that Celline was crying.

Celline waited another ten minutes after hearing her mum's bedroom door close before getting out of bed and pulling on the soft hand-knitted jumper her gran had made her, two Christmasses ago; before her hands had become too stiff and gnarled to hold the needles. She slipped her shoes back on and looked at her watch, it was nine-thirty, which meant there was enough time to walk to the beach, even with her gran's slow pace.

She slipped out of her room, checking that her mum's door was in fact closed before tip toeing down the stairs and along the hallway to her gran's room, where she found Cordelia ready to leave, sitting on her chair beside the bed.

Her gran's face lit up when she saw her granddaughter, and Celline went to help her get up.

"The letters are in my writing desk," she whispered to Celline. "Make sure your mother gets hers tomorrow morning, I don't want her to cause a fuss with the authorities."

"Okay, Gran," Celline whispered back. "You've got the necklace?" Cordelia nodded and patted her pocket, and Celline helped her gran to the door. They both crept down the hall to the front door, and slipped out into the moonlit night. Celline hadn't realised she was holding her breath until she gasped for air the moment the door was closed.

They made their way slowly down the hill, and Celline prayed that they wouldn't bump into anyone, or be spotted by a nosey neighbour looking out the window. She was relieved when they finally made it across the railway bridge and over the road to the concrete steps to the beach. Suddenly, a cold breeze whipped through their hair, making Celline and Cordelia shiver, though they were dressed warmly. The logical, rational part of Celline knew it was madness to let her grandmother enter the sea in the cold weather, but there was a stronger part of Celline that knew that the magic would keep her warm. And though she half hoped that the pearl necklace wouldn't contain enough magic to transform her gran, she knew in her heart that it did. And that her gran would indeed go home, for the final time.

When their feet hit the sand, Celline slipped off her shoes and kicked them to the side of the steps. She would retrieve them later. She bent down and her gran lifted one foot at a time so Celline could slip her shoes off, and she put them aside, next to hers.

Then they set off across the sand, following the moonlit path to the water's edge.

“Celline!’

Celline looked out to the dark horizon, at the sound of her name being called over the sea breeze. Her heart leapt when she saw Lir swimming towards them.

“Lir!” she called out, trying not to start crying again. But she realised that this would be the last time she saw him too. For a long while at least. She wasn’t sure how many pearls he possessed to be able to transform.

“I’m ready, my sweet child,” Cordelia said.

The freezing cold waves were gently lapping their toes, and Celline nodded. Cordelia took out the pouch, shook out the necklace, and handed it to her granddaughter, who undid the clasp, and then reached up around her gran’s neck to put it on her. When the clasp clicked shut, Celline felt a rush through her body, and all the hairs on her arms stood up under her thick jumper. She wrapped her arms around her gran’s ample middle and squeezed tight for a moment, and her gran hugged her back, her face in Celline’s long hair.

“I love you, Celline. More than I can explain.

And I love your mother too. But I am so, so very happy to be going home. I have missed it so."

Celline nodded, her face buried in her gran's cardigan. The waves hit their shins suddenly, and Celline gasped.

Cordelia gasped too, but for a different reason.

Celline let go and stepped back as her gran waded forward into the water, her hands grasped tightly around the single large pearl. Her steps quickened as the effect of the magic in the pearl necklace took hold. Finally, when she was nearly waist deep, she pulled off her cardigan and top, and dove into the water.

Ignoring the stinging cold of the water as it soaked her jeans, Celline waded forward, tears streaming down her cheeks.

When her gran resurfaced a few feet away, she blinked and squinted into the moonlight.

"Gran?" she called out, unable to believe her eyes.

Cordelia giggled and smoothed her long hair from her eyes. Her long, dark hair. That moments ago was completely white.

Her wrinkled face had smoothed out, and

Celline recognised her face from the old photos she had seen when she was younger.

"You're young again!" she exclaimed into the wind. "How?"

"Merfolk don't age, remember?" Lir called out, swimming towards Cordelia.

They embraced, and Lir leaned forward to whisper into Cordelia's ear. Celline couldn't hear what he said, but she saw her gran nod, and he handed her something.

"Are you going? Is this it?" she called out, her heart pounding, her eyes stinging with more tears.

Lir embraced Cordelia again, then her gran, now youthful and so very beautiful, turned to Celline and waved, a huge smile on her face.

"I will see you again, my sweet child!" she called out over the waves. "Come and see me in a few years, when you are older, and tell me everything that you have learnt and done."

Celline nodded, trying not to sob. "I will. I love you, Gran!"

Cordelia nodded and waved again, then dove under the water, her turquoise fin splashing up briefly, before disappearing. Celline swallowed hard, it felt like she had a huge pebble in her throat. Then she frowned. Why was Lir swimming to shore?

When he reached the shallows, she saw him slip something into his pocket, and then stood up, on human feet.

"Lir! You're becoming human again? For how long?"

When Lir was a few feet away, Celline averted her eyes, and took off her jumper to hand to Lir so he could cover up.

"I'm here to stay," he said, when he got closer. "I've given your grandmother my ring, so she can enter Sitnalta without my assistance. I have decided I would like to try to have a family. And that perhaps, I can be of some assistance to you and your mother, as she adjusts to the loss of your grandmother."

With those words, Celline looked back out to the water, and a heaviness hit her. Her gran was gone. She had gone home. After all these many years. But even knowing that she was where she wanted to go, it was hard for Celline to accept that she wouldn't see her every day.

Though it felt like she should have none left, more tears ran down Celline's red cheeks, and Lir reached out a hand and rested it on her shoulder.

"I will find a place to lay low, and in a few days or so, I will come to your house, and introduce myself to your mum as a long lost relative of your gran's, and say that she asked me to come. It will all be okay, I promise."

Celline nodded, but despite his reassurance, she wasn't sure that she would feel okay again.

She looked at her watch, time had slipped by and it was approaching midnight. She should get home

"Where will you go?" she asked Lir, shivering.

"Don't worry, I will figure it out," he replied. "Just get home. You will need some sleep for what is to come tomorrow."

Celline nodded. "I'll see you soon," she said, before heading across the sand to the steps where she'd left her shoes.

When she got to the edge of the beach, she picked up both pairs of shoes, tears welling up as she picked up her gran's worn, faded leather shoes.

How on earth was she going to get through the next day? She wished she could have become a mermaid too, and gone with her gran, so she wouldn't have to face her mother's sadness, and her own.

Her feet feeling like lead, she trudged home, and hoped that morning would come slowly.

CHAPTER NINETEEN

As Celline had feared, the next day was worse than any of her worst nightmares.

Despite Lir's encouragement to get some rest, Celline hadn't been able to sleep much, and had lay awake, just watching the sky get lighter outside her window, as the morning slowly crept upon her.

She had just glanced at her seashell clock, and saw it was seven am, when she heard a shout. She closed her eyes, and breathed deeply, knowing she was going to need all her strength.

"Mum?! Mum, where are you?"

Celline heard her mother's voice becoming panicked, as she heard her move about the house, searching for Cordelia.

Wishing she didn't have to, but knowing she had no choice, Celline got out of bed, pulled on her dressing gown, and headed downstairs to her gran's room, where she found her mum spinning around in panic, wondering where her mother had gone.

"Celline! Where's Gran? Her bed is made, but it doesn't even look like she slept in it!"

Celline shook her head. "She didn't."

Doris's eyes widened and she stopped spinning around. "What?" she said. "What do you mean?"

Celline walked by her to her gran's writing desk, and opened it with a slow creak. She picked up the two letters that lay there neatly, each bearing her name and her mother's.

She closed the writing desk and then turned to her mum. She held out the envelope, and hoped really hard that her gran had managed to explain her disappearance in a way that wouldn't make Doris immediately call the police.

"What is this?" her mum said, taking the envelope, and slipping her finger under the flap to open it. "Celline, what is going on?"

"Just read it," Celline said. She looked down at her own envelope, afraid to open it.

She watched her mother begin to read, and then sit down suddenly on her gran's bed, as through all the energy had suddenly left her body.

"She's gone where?!" her mother cried. "No, it's not possible, it's just a silly fairy-tale, it's not real." She looked up and Celline felt her own eyes filling in response to her mother's tears. "Celline, where is she? Where has she gone?"

"Home," Celline replied, the tears falling. "She really has gone home, Mum, I saw her myself. She transformed into a mermaid, and she dove into the water. She even became young again. Merfolk don't age like we do."

Celline couldn't quite believe that she was saying these words to her mother, who had never had much interest in the magical or paranormal. So she wasn't very surprised when her mum kept shaking her head, and then shouted "No!" before heading out of the room to call the police.

Celline sighed and sat on the bed to read her gran's letter to her mum. In all honesty, it did sound rather far-fetched. She heard her mum's hysterical voice reporting her gran missing and closed her eyes. It really had been too much to hope for, that her mum would believe them, and understand that Cordelia really had just gone home, and wasn't missing or in danger.

Celline breathed in deeply and wiped her tears with her sleeve. It was going to be a long day.

Several hours, dozens of cups of sweet tea and many hysterical phone calls to friends and family later, an exhausted Doris was sat at the breakfast bar, waiting by the phone for any news, while Celline put the kettle on to boil again.

The doorbell rang, piercing the tension-filled air, and Doris leapt of the stool and ran to the front door. Celline trailed after her, afraid of who it might be.

"Mrs Delmar?"

Celline saw the two police officers stood at the door, and her heart sank. She stood next to her mum and put her arm around her.

"Yes?" Doris replied, her voice shaking.

"I'm afraid that we have found some clothing, that appears it might belong to your mother."

"Clothing? Where?" Doris asked. Celline gripped her around the waist more tightly, feeling her mother starting to crumple.

"Washed up on the beach, I'm afraid. It would seem that you may have been right about her going into the water. We will be sending out search teams, but considering the temperatures last night…" the officer's voice trailed off. He didn't need to say anything else, it was clear that he didn't expect to find Cordelia alive.

Doris buckled to the floor suddenly, as her knees appeared to give way. Celline tried to catch her, but she was too heavy for her. One of the officers reached out to help pick her mum up, and they half-led, half-carried her to the lounge, as she sobbed uncontrollably.

Tears fell down Celline's face. This was exactly what she had feared. She knew her mum wouldn't believe that gran had really become a mermaid. Now she thought that Cordelia had drowned in the sea instead.

Once her mum was sat down, she thanked the

officers, and they left, leaving her wondering how to console her mother. She wished Lir were there, he would have known what to say. But instead, she was all on her own.

Six long days later, Celline was making her mum a cup of tea in the kitchen when she heard the doorbell. She frowned, and went to see who it was. When she opened the door, she nearly dropped the mug.

It was Lir. But he was no longer young and boyish-looking. He was a man.

"Lir?" she said, shocked by his appearance.

Lir smiled at her. "Hey, Celline," he said, his voice now an octave lower than it had been just a few days earlier. "How are you?"

After nearly a week of trying to comfort her mother, Celline found herself shrugging her shoulders, then bursting into tears.

Lir took the hot mug of tea from her hands, set it on the table by the door and hugged her tightly. "She hasn't taken it well?"

"No," Celline sobbed. "The police searched for gran for three days, but they have given up now. Mum thinks she's dead."

"Oh dear," Lir said, squeezing her tighter. "Shall I speak to her?"

Celline nodded. "Please."

Lir let her go and picked up the mug. "Where is she?"

Celline closed the door behind him and he followed her to the sun lounge, where Doris was sat in Cordelia's favourite chair, staring blindly out the window at the sea below.

"Doris?" Lir said softly, setting the mug down in front of her.

Doris blinked several times at the sound of a male voice and looked up at Lir, confusion on her face. "Who are you?" she asked, not rudely, but not very nicely either.

"I am Lir, I am Cordelia's nephew. She reached out to me a few days ago, and asked if I would come."

"A few days? You mean, you've heard from her? She's alive? You know where she is?"

Lir sat next to Doris and sighed. "No, she

contacted me before she left." He glanced up at Celline, who nodded. "Before she became a mermaid again and went home."

Doris sighed in disgust. "Are you being serious? Who are you, really? Someone my daughter has convinced to lie to me? Do I look foolish to you?"

"Mum," Celline said, sitting on her mum's other side, and taking her hand. "He really is your cousin, he is gran's nephew. Look at him, he has the same eyes, the same smile. Can't you see?"

Doris focused her gaze on Lir's face. His bright blue eyes shone, his black hair, once long and flowing, was now cut short, and a dark stubble adorned his chin. He smiled gently at Doris, and she began to cry.

"Yes, I can see it," she whispered. "But I cannot believe it. I cannot accept that my mother was a mermaid. It's preposterous."

"It's what she wanted you to believe," Celline said, squeezing her mum's hand. "Whether it's true or not, she wants you to believe that she is home, safe and happy." Celline sighed. "Can you not do that, for her? For me?"

Doris sighed. "Perhaps," she said.

Celline's heart lifted a little and she smiled at Lir. Perhaps there was hope yet, that her mum might just accept that magic existed after all.

Lir stayed for a while, and discussed arrangements that needed making. Despite not finding her gran, they would be holding a funeral, and they needed to invite family and friends to a small gathering at the house.

The only silver-lining to the sad occasion was that Celline would get to see her cousins, Lily and Kenny. She knew they would understand, even if her mum still refused to. She left her mum and Lir talking, and went upstairs to do some homework that Lauren had brought over for her. Lauren had felt bad that they had used two of her precious pearls that she could have used to visit her gran, but Celline had assured her that she was glad they had experienced what it was like to be mermaids.

She missed her friend, having stayed off school all week to take care of her mum, but she hoped she would be able to go back to school soon. She didn't want to get too behind on her schoolwork, and she knew her gran wouldn’t have wanted her to either.

Back in her room, she stroked the photo of her gran attached to her cork board above her desk, then she settled down to tackle the latest set of maths problems.

Chapter Twenty

Two weeks later, they held a small gathering to honour Cordelia's life. It was a very small affair, with just a few friends and the very few relatives that Celline had. Though she wondered how many more she might have, living under the waves in the golden city.

Though it felt like a heavy occasion, with the weight of her mother's grief still upon her, Celline was thrilled when her cousins arrived. They arrived on the train, and were staying at the hotel where her mum worked.

"Mick, Hazel! So good to see you both, thank you so much for coming, I really appreciate it."

Celline heard her mum greet Lily and Kenny's parents at the door and she put down the cloth she was using to dry the dishes in the kitchen and went to greet her cousins. Minutes later, they were safely up in her room, out of earshot of the adults.

"Oh, Celline! Are you okay?" Lily asked, throwing her arms around Celline and hugging her tightly.

Celline nodded and hugged her back. "I'm okay, it was really hard in the beginning, but now that Mum is starting to accept that Gran is gone, it's getting a bit easier."

"Did she really become a mermaid? And go home?" Kenny asked, his eyes huge.

Celline smiled at her younger cousin. "Yes, she did. She got really young too, merfolk don't age like we do."

"Will we get to meet your mer-cousin?" Lily asked. "Is he here?" She looked very excited at the prospect of meeting a real merman.

"Yes," Celline said, sitting down on her bed next to her cousins. "He is staying in town for a while until he decides where he wants to live.

He's made it a lot easier. I don't know why, but my mum seems to trust him. I think she may even be starting to believe him about Gran."

"I bet it's because he's magic," Kenny said wisely. "The faeries could get grownups to do what they wanted them to do."

Lily chuckled. "That's true!" She shook her head. "Imagine! We have mermaids in the family! What next? Dragons? Unicorns?"

Celline laughed, thinking of their conversation on the beachfront in the summer. It felt like such a long time ago. "Who knows?" she said. "Anything is possible."

"Celline!" Doris' voice filtered up the stairs and through the closed door.

Celline sighed. "I guess we'd better go and join everyone downstairs."

Even though she knew her gran was fine, it still felt like it was going to be difficult, being surrounded by people who had come to pay their respects and say goodbye.

Lily took Celline's hand in her and squeezed it. "Don't worry, we're here. We'll help you. After all, we know the truth. Auntie Cordelia is at home, healthy, happy and safe. Let's just go and talk about how much we love her."

Celline smiled at her cousin and nodded. Then the three of them went downstairs to join the adults.

Another full moon had slipped by, and suddenly, it seemed, Christmas had arrived, but neither Celline nor Doris had got into the spirit of the holiday that they usually both enjoyed.

Lir had moved in with them, and was living in the tiny box room, as neither Celline nor her mum had wanted to clear out Cordelia's belongings from her room yet. It seemed that despite having finally accepted that her mother was gone, Doris was still hoping that one day, Cordelia would appear again, and be back in their lives.

Two days after Christmas, Celline went into her gran's room, hoping to find some photos of her to put on her cork board, and found her mum curled up on the bed, crying softly.

"Mum?" she said, not wanting to startle her.

Doris looked up and beckoned her over,

so Celline joined her on bed. Doris pulled her in close, and they lay there for a few minutes, Celline listening to her mother's sniffles.

"It just hits me sometimes," she whispered. "That I will never see her again. That I didn't tell her how much I loved her. In fact, I can't remember the last time I said 'I love you' at all." Doris took in a shuddering breath. "I just miss her, so much."

Celline didn't respond. She thought of the two remaining magic pearls on her bracelet, and the letter her gran had left her, instructing her to use those pearls to visit in the future, when she was older.

Though she and Lir had told her mother that her gran was in the golden city, they hadn't mentioned that Celline still had two pearls, or that she also had her gran's ring, so she could get through the portal, to Sitnalta. Not that her mum would have believed them about that either.

But what if she could give her mother what she really needed? Give her the chance to see her mother again? To say goodbye, to see her happy, healthy and young again?

Before she could change her mind, Celline pulled away from her mum, and kissed her on the forehead. "I'll be back in a bit," she said, getting up off the bed and heading back to her own room. She went to her bedside table and took out the jewellery box that she kept her bracelet and ring in. She pulled out the jewellery kit and quickly took apart the bracelet again, carefully threading one of the still shining pearls onto a new bracelet, before adding a few more beads onto the original. She found a small Christmassy box that she kept trinkets in and emptied it out. She placed the bracelet in the box and closed it. Then she slipped on her own bracelet and the ring, and went back to her gran's room where her mother was still laying on the bed, crying.

"Mum," she said, sitting on the bed. "I have a late Christmas gift for you."

"Are you sure this is going to work?"

Celline smiled at her mother, who was stood next to her on the beach, her greying hair dancing in the breeze on the cold winter's night.

“Yes,” she said. “At least, I hope the pearl has enough to change you. It’s a super moon tonight, and Gran said those were stronger. You should go first though, just in case.”

Still with a look of disbelief on her face that she had allowed her daughter to convince her to go in the sea in the middle of winter, Doris took a deep breath, and waded into the water a few feet, gasping at the icy cold of the waves lapping at her ankles. She slipped on the bracelet Celline had made her with one of her pearls, held the pearl and then started gasping and grabbing at her throat.

“Go!” Celline said, pushing her further into the water and slipping on her own bracelet, on the same hand as her gran’s ring. She held onto the final magic pearl, and could feel herself beginning to transform, so she grabbed her mum’s hand and they both waded into the deeper water, before finally diving into the waves, and taking in beautiful deep breaths of oxygen.

Under the water, Celline’s mother turned to her, her eyes wide. “We’re mermaids!” she exclaimed. “Mermaids are real! You were right!”

Celline giggled, bubbles escaping from her mouth. “Yes we are, and I did try to tell you!”

Doris shook her head. “This is incredible!” She swam around for a few moments, and Celline laughed with joy at seeing her mother so playful and light, after being so heavy with sadness for the previous few months. “Am I dreaming?”

Celline grinned when her mother finally stopped twirling about. “No, you are not dreaming. Now, are you ready to go see Gran?”

Doris nodded, looking younger and more joyful than Celline had seen her look for a very long time. Celline waved for her mum to follow, then swam along the moonlit path, to the magical portal to Sitnalta, where she would see her gran again.

As if on cue, the dolphin arrived, and Doris giggled in delight as she reached out to touch its silky body, as they glided through the water together.

It hadn’t been long since Celline had last seen her grandmother, but she couldn’t wait to see her again. And she hoped that after seeing Cordelia one more time, her mum might finally find some peace, and be able to live fully again. Maybe, she would even be able to find the magic in life again, and who knew, perhaps she would find work she loved, or even someone new to love. But for now, Celline was just so very grateful she could give her mum this one gift, even if it meant giving up her future visits with her gran.

Her mother's happiness was definitely better than any of the Christmas gifts she had received. As were all of the memories she had of her gran, and the new memories she would make with her new friends, and her cousin, Lir.

Even though she might never become a mermaid again after this night, she would always be a mermaid at heart, and feel more at home in the sea than anywhere else. And she would continue to do what she could to help the merfolk, in any small way possible.

Because they were her family.

The statue with the shining blue opal became visible in the moonlight, and with the dolphin and her mother by her side, Celline swam towards it.

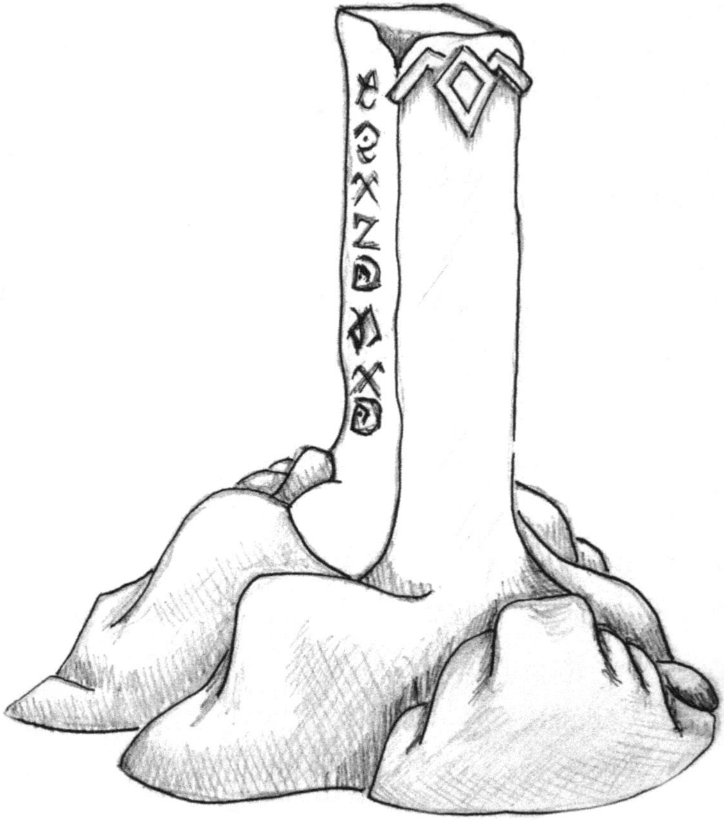

PROTECT SITNALTA!

If you loved The Magical Mermaid Portal, and would like to help the merfolk, please do look for local groups organising beach clean ups, and try to cut down on single plastic use as much as possible.

The setting for this book was inspired by a trip to Barmouth, in North Wales, where I saw a window display of a mermaid made from rubbish collected from the beach. Created by the Cambrian Water Guardians, it was made to bring awareness to the amount of rubbish that ends up in the waters, that endangers all who live there.

You can find the Cambrian Water Guardians on Facebook.

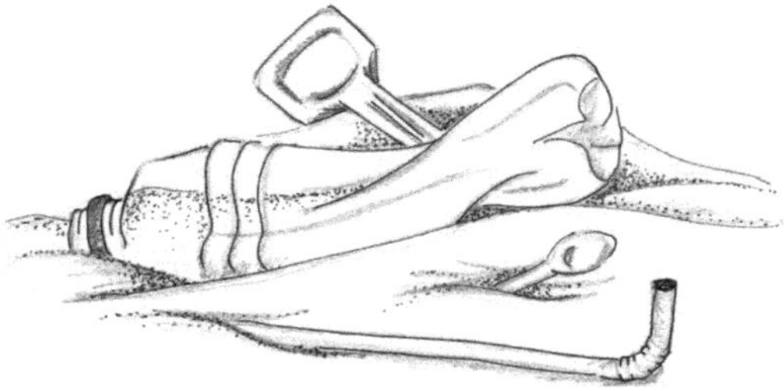

About the Artist

Lucja has made her home in the beautiful Wye Valley, where she and her husband have raised their two boys.

A lifelong artist, Lucja also owns a vegan skincare and soy candle business, *naturally wye.* She harvests the botanicals for her products from her very own garden.

naturallywye.co.uk

About the Author

Michelle lives in the UK, when she's not flitting in and out of other realms. She believes in faeries and unicorns and thinks the world needs more magic and fun.

Please feel free to write a review of this book. Michelle loves to get direct feedback, so if you would like to contact her, please e-mail **theamethystangel@hotmail.co.uk** or keep up to date by following her blog – **TwinFlameBlog.com.** You can also follow her on Instagram **@michellegordonauthor**

You can now become an Earth Angel Trainee:
earthangelacademy.co.uk

To sign up to her mailing list, visit:
michellegordon.co.uk

Lightning Source UK Ltd.
Milton Keynes UK
UKHW041100110722
405686UK00001B/55

9 781912 257430